Abby stared at him. "So—you seriously expect I would be willing to be your mistress?"

"Why not?" Luke spoke succinctly, and she clenched her fists so tightly, her nails dug into her palms.

"Just because I let you make love to me the last time you were here doesn't mean I'll do it again!" she retorted angrily, despising herself and him in equal measure.

"Well, forgive me," he said sarcastically. "Only it's hard to feel sympathy for a woman who's cheated on her husband in the past."

"You know nothing about my marriage to Harry."

"And I don't want to know," he retorted, reaching for his jacket. "Perhaps you're right. Perhaps I should get out of here."

"Perhaps you should," said Abby, striving for indifference.

But before Luke could grab his jacket and leave, his strong fingers trailed down her sleeve and flipped beneath the hem of her shirt. She tried to back away from him, but the temptation of Luke's touch was too much for her.

And when his hand spread against her bare midriff, warm and possessive against her soft flesh, every nerve in her body went on high alert. She wanted him to touch her, she admitted despairingly. Her limbs were melting in anticipation of his caress.

Without giving her a chance to break his hold, he pulled her down onto the sofa again and, pressing her back, covered her body with his.

Anne Mather and her husband live in the north of England in a village bordering the county of Yorkshire. She's been making up stories since she was in primary school and would say that writing is a huge part of her life. Anne's written over 160 novels, and her books have appeared on both the *New York Times* and *USA TODAY* bestseller lists. You can email her at mystic-am@msn.com.

Books by Anne Mather

Harlequin Presents

Innocent Virgin, Wild Surrender
His Forbidden Passion
The Brazilian Millionaire's Love-Child
A Forbidden Temptation

Latin Lovers

Mendez's Mistress

Queens of Romance

Bedded for the Italian's Pleasure
The Pregnancy Affair

The Greek Tycoons

The Greek Tycoon's Pregnant Wife

For Love or Money

Stay Through the Night

Wedlocked!

Jack Riordan's Baby

Foreign Affairs

In the Italian's Bed
Sleeping with a Stranger
The Virgin's Seduction

Visit the Author Profile page at Harlequin.com for more titles.

Anne Mather

—

MORELLI'S MISTRESS

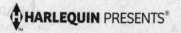

HARLEQUIN PRESENTS®

ISBN-13: 978-0-373-13908-8

Morelli's Mistress

First North American Publication 2016

Copyright © 2016 by Anne Mather

Printed in U.S.A.

™ www.Harlequin.com

MORELLI'S MISTRESS

To Sally Fairchild, for her encouragement, and to my editor, Joanne Grant, for making the book live.

PROLOGUE

LUKE NOTICED HER as soon as he went into the wine bar.

She was anchored to a stool next to the bar, a cocktail glass with slices of fruit curving over the rim and a tiny coloured parasol propped inside beside her hand.

She didn't appear to have drunk much of the liquid in the glass. She was simply sitting there, staring into space, ignoring the loud voices and even louder music that filled the overcrowded room.

'Oh, man, she's hot!'

Ray Carpenter, who had followed Luke into the bar, was instantly attuned to what had drawn his partner's attention. Coming abreast of the other man, he threw an arm about Luke's shoulders.

'Do you think she's on her own?' He paused. 'Nah, she's too good-looking to be buying her own drinks.'

'You think?'

Luke didn't want to have this conversation. For the first time that evening, he wished Ray weren't with him. But they'd been finishing up the plans for their latest development project and it would have been churlish not to accept the other man's invitation to go for a drink.

The choice of wine bar had been Ray's, of course. Luke would have preferred to go to the pub across the street from their offices in Covent Garden. But Ray had insisted they deserved a celebratory cocktail, so here they were.

And just then, the girl turned her head and saw them. Or at least Luke was fairly sure she had, anyway. He didn't think her eyes moved beyond his heavy-lidded gaze, and for a heart-stopping moment they simply stared at one another. Then Luke threw off Ray's arm and moved towards her.

She was good-looking, and fairly tall, judging by the long slender legs that crossed at the knee. Her face was oval and she had a rather attractive nose. Above the kind of mouth most girls could only dream of.

Her hair was silvery blonde and she was wearing a gauzy wrap over a black vest. Her skirt was short and red, black tights ending in high-heeled pumps, one of which dangled enticingly from one swinging foot.

Luke halted beside her and then said quietly, 'Hi. Can I buy you a drink?'

The girl, who had resumed her contemplation of the room, lifted her glass without looking at him again. 'I have a drink.'

'Okay.'

Luke wished there were a free stool beside her that he could casually score. But the guy who was sitting next to her was evidently on a bender, huddled over a clutch of beer bottles on the bar.

'Are you alone?'

It wasn't the most original thing to say, and the girl glanced up at him, her lips turning down. 'No,' she said flatly.

'I'm with them.' She indicated a group of women gyrating around the tiny dance floor. 'It's a hen party,' she added, with a dismissive shrug.

'And you didn't want to dance?'

'No.' She moved the parasol to the other side of her glass and took a sip. 'I don't dance.'

'Don't—or won't?' Luke queried softly, and she blew out a rueful breath.

'I'm not in the mood for dancing,' she replied, concentrating on her glass. 'Look, don't you have someone else to talk to? I'm afraid I'm not very good company.' She grimaced. 'Go and ask the bride-to-be. She'll tell you. I'm just the skeleton at the feast.'

Luke pulled a wry face. 'If you say so.'

He flicked his fingers to get the attention of the bartender and ordered a beer for himself and a mojito for Ray. 'That guy over there.' He indicated the other man, who had apparently already found himself a willing companion. Then, when his beer was delivered, he swallowed half the bottle in one gulp. 'I needed that.'

The girl ignored him, but the guy on the stool next to her uttered a loud belch and got to his feet before stumbling away. Luke hooked his hip over the stool he'd vacated. 'Do you mind?' he asked mildly, and the girl at last turned to give him an old-fashioned look.

'It's a free country,' she said. And, as if regretting her earlier attitude, she added, 'Thank goodness, he's gone.'

Then, with a change of heart, 'Do you think he'll be all right?'

'I think so.' Luke grinned, and to his surprise the girl grinned back. 'Are you sure you won't have another drink?'

'Well, maybe a white wine,' she said, pushing the cocktail glass aside, and Luke noticed she was wearing a ring on her left hand. But on her middle finger. 'Liz got me this, but it's not really my thing.'

'Liz being?'

'Oh, the bride-to-be.' The girl frowned.

'That's her over there wearing the rabbit ears and the tutu over her pants.'

Luke grimaced. 'How could I miss her?' Then when the bartender reappeared, he ordered a glass of chardonnay. 'I'm Luke Morelli, by the way. What's your name?'

'A—Annabel,' she replied, after a moment's hesitation, and Luke suspected she had been going to say something else. The wine was delivered and she took a sip from the glass, her eyes lighting with pleasure. 'Hmm, this is nice.'

Luke thought so, too, only he wasn't talking about his beer. It was months since he'd felt such an immediate attraction to a girl. The women he met in the course of his work were as interested in a man's bank balance as what he had in his pants.

'Tell me about yourself,' he said. 'Do you work in London?'

'I do research. At the university,' she said. 'How about you?' She studied his lean, muscular frame, his dark navy suit and his matching shirt.

He'd removed his tie, as a gesture to informality, but that was all. 'Do you work for the Stock Exchange? You look as if you do.'

'I—work for the local authority,' said Luke, defending himself with the knowledge that their latest commission was building a new set of offices for the district council. 'Sorry to disappoint you.'

'Oh, you don't.' She smiled. 'I'm quite relieved. So many people think the Exchange is hallowed ground.'

'Not me,' said Luke staunchly.

'So what do you like to do when you're not working?' she asked, and for a while they discussed the merits of playing sports over attending the theatre. In actual fact, Luke liked both, but it was more fun to present an argument than to agree.

By the time the hen party had drunk enough, and exhausted themselves enough, to come and see what she was doing, Abby was almost disappointed.

She'd been enjoying herself for the first time in she didn't know how long. She seldom went out these days, unless Harry needed a chauffeur, preferring to avoid the kind of places he chose to go.

She'd met Harry Laurence at a friend's wedding, and when they'd first started going out together, Abby had felt she was the luckiest girl in the world. Harry had made her feel special, spoiling her with expensive gifts, taking care of her in a way that, being the only child of a single parent, she'd never experienced before.

But after their marriage things had changed. She'd realised that the character he'd adopted when other people—particularly her mother— were around was totally different from the man he really was.

She'd learned, almost from the start, not to question his whereabouts. She suspected he saw other women, but when she'd been foolish enough to challenge him on it, he'd flown into a rage.

She knew she should get a divorce. She used to tell herself that if he ever laid a hand on her, she would leave. But then, two years ago, when Abby was seriously thinking of filing for a divorce, her mother fell ill.

Annabel Lacey had developed a serious physical condition that required twenty-four-hour nursing. She needed the professional services of a comfortable nursing home, one which only Harry with his stock-market salary could provide.

And Abby had known then that, until her mother was well again, her life was on hold...

'We're leaving,' Liz Phillips said now, bringing Abby back to the present. She looked admiringly at Abby's companion. 'Who's this?'

'Um—this is Luke,' murmured Abby awkwardly, as he got politely up from his stool.

'Nice to meet you,' Luke said, smiling in Liz's direction.

'Likewise.' Liz gave him a flirtatious look. 'Well, we're going on to the Blue Parrot. Do you two want to come along?'

'Oh...' Abby slipped down from her stool, too, smoothing the short skirt down over her hips as she did so. 'I don't think so. I might just call it a night, if you don't mind?'

Liz's eyes drifted irresistibly back to Luke. 'I don't blame you,' she said as one of the other girls pushed to the front of the group. 'He's gorgeous!'

'Liz!' said Abby in embarrassment, but she wasn't listening.

'Hi. I'm Amanda,' said the other girl eagerly. 'No wonder Abs has been keeping you to herself.'

'I haven't—that is—' Abby looked at Luke in some consternation. 'We've only just met.'

'What she means is, she didn't know I was coming,' Luke amended lightly. 'But in the circumstances, I'm sure you'll understand that I'll be taking—Abs—home.'

'Oh, sure. Lucky Abs,' remarked a third girl with a knowing grin. 'But if you ever need a shoulder to cry on.'

'I'll keep that in mind,' he said, ignoring Abby's expression, and, after a few more embarrassing quips, the half-dozen or so members of the hen party departed.

After they'd gone, Abby glanced anxiously about her. 'Why did you let them think we were together?' she demanded, bending to pick up her handbag, which she'd wedged beside the stool when she sat down. 'We hardly know one another.'

'That can be remedied,' he replied, helping her extract the strap of her bag from the footrest. His hand brushed hers as he did so, and Abby felt an electric shock of awareness shoot up her arm. 'Come on. I'll give you a ride home. It's the least I can do.'

'How do you know I don't have a car?' she countered, knowing she should refuse his offer, and he arched a lazy brow.

'Do you?'

'No.'

'So why are we arguing? I promise I'm not a thief or a pervert.'

'And I'm expected to take your word for that?'

Abby looked up into his lean dark face. Liz was right, she thought. He was gorgeous. Tall, with a lean yet muscular body, dark-haired and olive-skinned, with curiously tawny eyes that were presently assessing her with a certain amount of amusement as well as interest.

'You could ask my friend over there,' he said, indicating the man he'd bought a drink for.

'And he's going to disagree, isn't he?' said Abby drily.

Then, with a fatalistic shrug, she said, 'Okay. I'll get my coat.'

'Give me the ticket and I'll get it for you,' said Luke. And Abby, who had been seriously considering slipping out the back way, expelled a resigned breath.

CHAPTER ONE

ABBY TOOK THE last batch of blueberry muffins out of the oven, inhaling their delicious fragrance as she set the tray on the counter nearby.

She unloaded the muffins onto a cooling tray and checked that the coffee machine had been filled that morning. The scones she'd baked earlier were just waiting to be transferred into a basket.

She still had to fill the small pots with jam, but the creamers could wait until she had her first customer of the day.

She also had cupcakes to bake, but they were mixed and ready. She had only to separate them into their cases before popping them in the oven.

She wondered when she'd developed such a love of baking. Not while she was married to Harry; that was for sure.

In those days, she'd spent all her free time working, saving for the day when she could support both her mother and herself.

Unfortunately that day had never come.

She sighed.

Nevertheless, she felt a pleasant sense of satisfaction as she looked about her. The small café, with the bookshop she'd introduced, was everything she'd hoped it would be. Her mother would have loved it, she thought wistfully. But she'd died of motor neurone disease just two years after entering the nursing home.

Abby had discovered the small café, which had previously been run by two sisters, now retired, when she'd been trawling the Internet. Until then the idea of moving out of London had only been a pipe dream. But the café in Ashford-St-James had been available for rent, and it had seemed an inspiration. When she'd learned it also had living accommodation, Abby hadn't hesitated before applying for the tenancy.

Then, when her divorce from Harry had been made final, she'd bought herself a bottle of Pinot Noir and had a private celebration. Before packing up the bedsit, where she'd been living since she'd left Harry, and moving herself and Harley, her mother's golden retriever, to this small Wiltshire town.

She supposed she must have always dreamed about running her own café. And the owner, an elderly man called Mr Gifford, had had no objections to her desire to modernise the interior to suit her needs. She'd used what little money she'd saved to give the place a makeover. It looked much different now from the rather dingy tearoom she'd first encountered.

To begin with, she'd bought the cakes and pastries she served with the coffee from the wholesalers. But then, one day she'd tried her hand at making muffins, and the results had been so good, she'd never looked back.

But she'd also discovered that the café on its own didn't generate a huge income. Which might have been why the sisters who'd run it before her had had to give it up. Although it had a steady clientele, they didn't get a lot of tourists in Ashford-St-James.

Which was why she'd had the idea of adding a bookshop. There were a lot of older people living in the area, who found visiting the bookshops in Bath just too much trouble. How much easier it was to come out for a coffee and browse the bookshelves when you'd finished. Abby was sure that many of the single men who used the café wouldn't have done so without the added attraction of choosing a bestseller.

And in the last four years, she'd made a good life for herself here, she thought contentedly. She was happier than she'd been since before her marriage. She and Harley suited one another.

Okay, her friends in London thought she was a fool to settle in a backwater like Ashford.

But after working every hour God sent when she was employed in the English department at the university, Abby appreciated being her own boss. She was able to set her own schedule, with no one looking over her shoulder and checking her work.

Leaving the huge Italian coffee machine, which had been her biggest and most successful outlay, bubbling away behind her, Abby walked through to the small bookshop.

A young mother who lived in the town, and wanted employment to fit in with her six-year-old's needs, worked with her. But Lori didn't turn up until nine o'clock, after delivering her daughter to the local primary school.

At present, everywhere was quiet, and Abby wandered happily amongst the shelves, restoring books that had been misplaced, and generally admiring the result.

Her peaceful reverie was broken by someone hammering on the outer door. Glancing at her watch, Abby saw that it was barely seven o'clock and she didn't open the café until half past.

It had to be an emergency, she thought, though what kind of an emergency she couldn't imagine. Unless Harley had somehow got out of the flat upstairs and had been found roaming the streets of the small country town.

That would be an emergency!

* * *

Luke Morelli stepped out of his current girl-friend's basement apartment, and climbed the steps to the street above.

It was cool in Grosvenor Mews, but he breathed a sigh of relief. He hadn't been lying when he'd told the young woman he'd been see-ing for the past couple of weeks that he had meetings planned for this morning. And, as a consequence, he wouldn't be able to drive her to the photo shoot in Bournemouth as she'd hoped.

Besides, their association was getting too se-rious. Luke seldom, if ever, continued a relation-ship beyond a couple of weeks. Occasionally, when he indulged in a little introspection, he put it down to the fact that his mother had walked out on his father when he was just a boy. Oli-ver Morelli had been shattered at this betrayal, and Luke had determined then never to suffer the same fate.

And he'd never been tempted. Except on one less-than-memorable occasion.

He strode out of the Mews now and along the Embankment. It was a beautiful morning; spring was definitely in the air. It was surpris-ingly warm, even at this early hour, and he de-cided to walk for a while before heading to his office.

The headquarters of the Morelli Corporation

were in Canary Wharf, a far cry from the pokey premises in Covent Garden where he and Ray Carpenter had started the company. Of course, Ray was long gone these days. He'd decided to take his share of the business and move to Australia. He appeared to be doing pretty well, Luke had thought, when he'd visited him last year. But as Ray had said, not without a certain degree of good-natured envy, he was no longer in Luke's league.

Jacob's Tower, where the Morelli offices were situated, occupied a prominent position in Bank Street. There were several other companies leasing property in the building, with a branch of a well-known string of luxury hotels occupying the first three floors.

Luke's office was on the penthouse floor, with an adjoining apartment that he used on occasion. But he also owned a house in Belgravia, an elegant Georgian property, that he'd invested in before the price of houses in London had hit the roof.

Luke attended the weekly board meeting and then informed his secretary that he was leaving for the rest of the day. 'I'm going to drive down to Wiltshire, to take another look at those properties in Ashford-St-James,' he told her, gathering the necessary files from his desk. 'And I promised my father I'd call in on him. I haven't seen him since we met in the solicitor's office when Gifford died.'

'Very well, Mr Morelli.' Angelica Ryan, an efficient middle-aged woman in her fifties, who had been with him for the past ten years, nodded in agreement. 'Will you be back tomorrow?'

'I expect so.' Luke pulled a wry face. 'I'll let you know if anything comes up.'

Responding to the uncompromising summons, Abby left the area devoted to the bookshop, and hurried across the café to the door. It was a reinforced glass door, although recently, on the advice of the local police constable, Abby had had an iron grill installed inside. But she could still see who her visitor was, and her heart sank at the sight of Greg Hughes.

Greg Hughes owned the photography studio next door. Abby assumed it had once been a thriving business, but these days, with amateur photographers and cameras in mobile phones, she wondered how he made a living.

To her regret, she didn't like Greg. She'd tried to when she'd first moved into the café, but he'd instantly struck her as a smarmy character, always wanting to know all her personal details.

Harley didn't like him either. The retriever, always such a placid animal, usually growled when Greg came onto the premises. Harley wasn't permitted to have the run of the food area, of course, but just occasionally he managed to hide away behind the shelves of books.

'Greg?' Abby said now, the inquiry evident in her voice. 'Is something wrong?'

'Damn right something's wrong,' declared her visitor irritably. 'Haven't you read your mail today?'

Abby frowned. 'The mail hasn't arrived yet,' she said, feeling obliged to invite him inside. His breath smelt strongly of garlic and it wasn't pleasant this early in the morning.

'Well, did you read yesterday's mail, then?' demanded Greg, his chubby frame fairly quivering with indignation. 'As you probably noticed, I was away at a craft fair yesterday, and I didn't bother checking my post until this morning.'

Abby sighed. She refrained from telling him that she hadn't noticed that his shop was closed. He got so few clients, it was difficult to tell when he was open and when he was not.

Besides, in all honesty, she rarely bothered reading through the pile of bills and circulars that came through her door on a daily basis. She saved them for when she was feeling confident that this month she'd make a profit.

'I'm afraid I must have forgotten,' she said, unable to imagine what might have got him so steamed. 'Do you want a coffee?'

'Oh, thanks.'

Taking her at her word, Greg appropriated one of the tables in the window, leaving Abby to bring his coffee to him.

Then, when he'd added cream and sugar to his liking, he said, 'So you haven't heard that old man Gifford has died and his son is selling this row of businesses to a developer.'

Abby's jaw dropped. 'No.' She stared at him disbelievingly. 'When did he die? Why weren't we informed?'

'Apparently, it was quite recently. Well, it would be, wouldn't it? I saw the old man in town about three months ago.'

Abby shook her head. 'But can his son do this? I mean, I've got a lease.'

'And when does your lease run out?'

'Um—in about six months, I think. But I was hoping to extend it.'

'As we all were,' said Greg grimly. 'But it's not going to happen.'

Abby's heart sank. 'But this is my home as well as my business.'

'Tell me about it.' Greg took a generous mouthful of his coffee, smacking his lips with pleasure. 'Hmm, that's good.'

Abby couldn't believe this was happening. 'But what can we do?'

'I haven't given it a lot of thought yet,' said

Greg, swallowing more of his coffee. 'We need to speak to the other shopkeepers first. I suppose we could contact Martin Gifford and ask him if he'd consider a raise in the rents instead.'

Abby frowned. 'Do you think he might?'

'No.' Greg grimaced. 'It's about as likely as the developer withdrawing his offer.'

'Like that's going to happen.' Abby looped her hands behind her neck, walking agitatedly about the room. 'Developers don't do that sort of thing.'

'You said it.'

Greg finished his coffee and pushed his cup across the table towards her. But if he hoped she might offer him a refill, he was disappointed. Abby was already thinking she would have to conserve what few assets she had. She knew Mr Gifford's son was unlikely to pay her for the improvements she'd made to the café when he intended on demolishing it.

Turning back to Greg, she said, 'Do you know who the developers are?'

'Why? Are you seriously thinking of appealing to their better nature?'

'Of course not.' Abby was impatient. 'I'm just curious, that's all. It's not as if Ashford-St-James is a hive of industry.'

'No, but it lacks a decent supermarket. According to the solicitor, whose letter I read this morning, the plan is to build a block of rental apartments above the retail area.'

Abby expelled a weary breath. 'I wonder if they'll offer us accommodation in the new apartments, at a reduced rate, of course.'

'Well, I don't need accommodation,' said Greg a little smugly. 'I bought my modest bungalow when property was cheap.' He paused. 'And you could always stay with me until you find yourself somewhere else to live, Abby. I doubt if you could afford the rents the Morelli company is likely to charge.'

Abby's breath stalled. 'Did you say—Morelli?' she asked tensely.

'Yes.' Greg frowned. 'Do you know them?'

'I know—of them,' admitted Abby, a feeling of nausea invading her stomach.

And with it came another thought. Dear God, did Luke Morelli know she was renting one of these properties? Was this an attempt on his part to take his revenge?

Abby lay awake, staring dully at the light from the street lamps outside filtering through the curtained windows. Harry was snoring peacefully beside her, having completed his masculine domination of her in the usual way.

All the same, his anger had been totally unexpected. He'd known where she was going;

known who she was with. Yet he'd still managed to ruin her evening when she'd got home.

Her first indication of his mood had come as soon as she'd walked into the living room of the apartment.

'Where the hell have you been?' he'd demanded, snagging the strap of the bag Abby had had slung over her shoulder. She'd staggered a little when he'd used it to haul her towards him.

'You know where I've been,' she'd said, refusing to let him see he'd shocked her. 'It was Liz's hen night. You said I should go.'

'Only because I didn't want your mother getting on my case again about me neglecting you,' he'd retorted, pushing his face close to hers. 'You stink of alcohol. How many drinks have you had?'

'Just one,' Abby had said defensively. She'd refused to count the cocktail, which she'd only tasted. 'A glass of wine. Hardly in your league, am I?'

She'd barely avoided the hand Harry had raised towards her. 'Don't you speak to me like that,' he'd snarled, and she'd wondered how much longer she could live like this. 'I asked you a civil question and I expect a civil answer. Or would you like Mummy to hear what an ungrateful girl you are?'

Abby had wrenched her bag away from him. Her mother was too ill to be upset by their troubles. When Abby had seen her the previous day, she'd been shocked by how frail she had become. And Harry knew that. That was why he always used her mother's health as a lever to get his own way.

Whatever, there was no point in trying to reason with him in this mood. And, in all honesty, she had been feeling guilty. She shouldn't have let Luke Morelli drive her home.

But for heaven's sake, she'd done nothing wrong. And it had been so nice for once, just to talk to a man who seemed to enjoy her company; who didn't treat her like his servant, or worse.

'So where did you go?'

Abby had been heading for the door, but she should have known Harry wasn't finished with her yet.

'Just the Parker House,' she'd replied, identifying the wine bar. 'You knew where we were going. I told you before I left.'

'So you didn't go on anywhere else?'

'Um—no.' But Abby had hesitated, and that had been a mistake.

'So you did go on somewhere else.' Harry had been on her in an instant. 'And you weren't going to tell me. Why?'

Abby had prayed the heat she could feel in her bones wasn't filling her cheeks. 'I didn't go anywhere else,' she'd insisted wearily. 'The others were going on to the Blue Parrot, but I didn't want to go.'

'Why not? Had you found someone more interesting at the Parker House?' Harry's eyes had bored into hers. 'If you've been with another man—'

'I haven't.' But Abby had felt herself trembling even so. 'I was tired, that's all. I wanted to come home.'

'So how did you get home? I thought they'd hired a minibus.'

'They did.' Abby had swallowed. 'I just— called a taxi.'

'Good idea.' Harry had grasped her wrist then, and pulled her into his arms. His own breath had smelt suspiciously sweet, his thick lips nuzzling her neck. 'I'm tired, too, baby,' he'd whispered, his hands roaming possessively over her breasts. 'What say we both go to bed?'

Luke Morelli sat staring at his laptop computer, studying the webpage that listed all the London universities.

God, there were dozens of them, he saw frustratedly. And he had no idea what kind of re-

search the girl he was looking for had been doing.

He scowled. It was almost a week since he and Ray had visited the wine bar where he'd met Annabel; almost a week since he'd driven her home. He didn't know why, but he hadn't been able to put her out of his mind, and it bugged the hell out of him that, although he'd given her his number, she hadn't bothered to call.

All he knew for certain was that she worked at one of the universities. And that her name was Annabel, although that was open to question, too. The other girls had called her Abs, which was surely short for Abigail. Or Abby, if he wanted to confuse the situation even more.

There was always the chance that if he went back to the wine bar, he'd see her. But she hadn't struck him as the kind of girl who frequented bars on a regular basis. He knew the building where he'd dropped her off, but there must have been about forty apartments in the block, and he didn't have a clue as to her surname.

He sighed. He honestly didn't know what it was about her that intrigued him. She was an attractive girl, yes, tall and slim, with silvery blonde hair that she wore straight to her shoul-

ders. But he'd known a lot of beautiful women, so that wasn't it.

She had been excessively slim, he mused, remembering how the bones of her shoulders had jutted through her vest when he'd helped her on with her jacket. Yet she hadn't struck him as the kind of girl who was overly concerned about her looks.

Ray Carpenter came into the office at that moment, pausing to glance over Luke's shoulder at the computer. 'What're you doing, man?' he asked, peering at the screen.

'Do you mind?' Luke cast an impatient look up at his partner. 'I'm checking something out, that's all.'

'Checking something out, or checking someone out?' suggested Ray shrewdly. 'You're looking at a university website, right? Didn't you tell me that girl you took home the other evening worked at a university?'

Luke's jaw compressed. 'What if I did?'

'Well, I'd say you're trying to get in touch with her. Where does she work?'

Luke's scowl deepened. 'I don't know.'

Ray gave a snort. 'But you know where she lives.'

'I know the block of apartments, but I don't know which one.'

'So go look at the list of tenants. They al-

ways have lists of tenants in the lobbies of these places, you know that.'

'Yeah.'

Luke cleared the webpage and closed the laptop. He had no desire to tell Ray that he didn't even know the girl's surname.

He'd been so eager not to offend her, he hadn't even kissed her goodnight.

But he'd wanted to. That luscious mouth of hers had been an almost irresistible temptation. And she'd smelled so good, too; soft feminine scents that had lingered in his car long after he'd dropped her off. Dammit, he thought, he was smitten. And that was something that had never happened to him before.

Thankfully, Ray dropped the subject and their discussion turned to the projects they were currently working on. Ray had spent the day in Milton Keynes. He liked the hands-on approach of checking on the site managers, while Luke had had a meeting with a real-estate agent concerning a property they were interested in buying north of the city.

The Covent Garden office was no longer big enough to accommodate the business. Their team of architects and designers, accountants and sales personnel, and all the usual administrative staff who made up Morelli and Carpenter Development, needed room to expand. It *was an intoxicating prospect and Luke was soon distracted by describing the run-down building he'd seen, which they could renovate to their own design.*

But later that evening, leaving the office, he couldn't prevent himself from turning towards Chelsea. It occurred to him, as he drove across Vauxhall Bridge, that the block of apartments where Annabel lived could be categorised as luxurious. Was she wealthier than he'd imagined? Was that why she hadn't bothered giving him a call. Or did she simply share the apartment with one or two of the girls he'd met the other night?

Which might make finding her address even more difficult.

Abby was standing at the living-room window, watching the rain trickling down the panes. It was early evening, but it was already getting dark, the overhanging clouds drenching the neat box hedges that surrounded Chandler Court.

Harry had called to say he might be late, but Abby never took anything for granted. He'd been known to make such a statement before, and then turn up half an hour later.

He'd suggested she should have her supper, but the chicken casserole was still sitting, untouched, on a low heat in the oven. Abby wasn't hungry. She was seldom hungry these days. She knew her mother worried that she was getting too thin, but food had become something of an anathema to her.

She'd intended to go and see her mother to-night, but the nurse had called earlier to say Mrs Lacey had had a bad day and was now rest-ing. Which meant she'd been sedated, guessed Abby uneasily. There were few days now when her mother was strong enough to conduct a con-versation for more than a couple of minutes.

She saw the car as soon as it turned into the grounds of the complex.

It was a distinctive vehicle, sleek and power-ful like its owner. Its dark green bodywork was only visible because it had stopped beneath one of the floodlights that switched on as soon as a car entered the grounds.

How did she know it was Luke Morelli's car? It was just a feeling she had, a sixth sense, that warned her this could mean trouble.

Pressing her fingers to her lips, Abby won-dered what she should do. There was no need to panic, she told herself. He didn't even know her name. But what if, after leaving her the other evening, he'd gone on to the Blue Par-rot, and someone there—another member of the hen party, perhaps—had given him that infor-

mation? It was a long shot, sure, and she was probably flattering herself that he'd been that interested. But could she take the risk?

No!

Glancing behind her, at the steel and chrome furnishings of the living room, Abby wondered if Luke would believe how much she hated living here. Would he understand why she had to stay, at the mercy of a man who didn't love her, but who enjoyed controlling her? That she stayed to give her mother the treatment Abby couldn't afford herself?

She doubted it. And right now, she needed to get rid of him.

She grabbed her jacket as she passed through the foyer, hauling out a pair of boots and shoving her feet inside. Then she cast a swift glance at her reflection. The black velvet lounging suit she was wearing wasn't really warm enough to go outside on an October evening. Particularly when it was raining and she didn't have an umbrella. But she didn't have time to change.

The apartment was on the sixth floor, and she took the lift down, praying that Harry wouldn't decide to call it a night and come home early. She could imagine his reaction if he caught her talking to a strange man in the lobby.

To her relief, there was no sign of Harry or Luke Morelli. Was she wrong? Were Luke's rea-

*sons for being here nothing to do with her, after
all? It might not even be Luke, she reminded
herself optimistically. The car he drove was
probably duplicated a dozen times throughout
the metro area.*

*She decided she would just peek outside and
see if the car had gone. It meant passing the
desk of the doorman, but happily McPhelan was
ensconced in the back room, watching the TV.
Only visitors to the apartments apparently war-
ranted a once-over from him.*

Thank God!

CHAPTER TWO

LUKE HAD DECIDED to leave his visit to Ashford-St-James until the next morning.

When he'd arrived at Oliver Morelli's home in Bath, he'd discovered that his father expected him to stay the night, and he hadn't wanted to disappoint him.

Besides, his visit to the properties in South Road was intended to be anonymous. How much easier it would be to browse the small shops his agent had described to him in the morning, without arousing any protests from their occupants.

Luke himself had never been to Ashford-St-James before. He'd only learned of the possible opportunity for developing the site from his father.

Charles Gifford, the owner of the properties, had been an old golfing partner of Oliver Morelli's. When he'd died, Gifford's son had wasted no time in informing his father's solicitor that as soon as probate was granted he was going to sell the row of shops in Ashford.

Prior knowledge had given Luke an advantage. And, although it was a small development compared to the work the Morelli Corporation undertook these days, Luke had sensed that Oliver Morelli wanted to feel he was contributing to his son's success.

Which was why the five businesses in question had been given six months' notice. It had also been Luke's father's suggestion that the tenants be given a decent interval of time to find themselves other accommodation.

Not that that was going to be easy, thought Luke, deciding to park his car in the centre of town and explore the place on foot. From what he'd heard, the shops in South Road were small concerns, more suited to the last century than this.

As far as he could see, the stores in High Road were upmarket clothes shops and jewellers. There were one or two phone outlets and a couple of coffee shops, but nothing along the lines of the businesses his father had described to him.

Conversely, there appeared to be few food shops. He could quite see why the local council were in favour of building a supermarket.

Nevertheless, it was an attractive place, the

mellow stonework of a church with its bell tower providing a focal point. The church stood beside a park, where a small lake provided a home for a family of ducks. Although it was early in the season, there were flowers already blooming in the planters that edged the market square, and the trees in the park had most of their foliage.

It was all very old English and very civilised. The kind of place that was attracting newcomers from London. People who were eager to escape the rat race; who wanted a slower pace of living, without losing all the benefits of the city.

Luke left his car near the town centre and strolled along the main street to where South Road ran at right angles to the high street. His father had given him directions and it was easy to find the row of properties Luke had taken an option on.

According to the details Luke had been given, there was a gift shop, a shop that sold woollens, a photo studio, and a bridal outfitters. The fifth property was a café-cum-bookshop, which the solicitor had told him was probably the most successful, financially speaking.

Luke crossed the road at the lights and strolled past the first of the shops. This was the bridal shop, with an extravagant lace wedding dress occupying the central position in a window full of bridal gear.

The photo studio was next door, its window draped with a purple backdrop in front of which resided a single digital camera.

At least it was a digital camera, thought Luke, wondering if people still sat for formal portraits these days. Maybe the photographer made his living filming weddings or christenings. Perhaps he teamed up with the bridal outfitters, and they kept each other informed.

He grinned to himself, and moved on to the next business. This was the café, with the gift shop beyond. The gift shop appeared to have a window filled with an array of soft toys and knick-knacks that any serious shopper would call junk. But obviously some people liked it or the shop would have closed before now.

Luke wasn't much interested in the woollen shop, so he paused outside the café-cum-book-shop.

He glanced at his watch. It was after ten. He supposed he could legitimately call in for a coffee. The place was called Harley's, and there was an appetising array of scones and cakes visible on trays at the counter.

There was also a number of bistro tables and chairs, several of which were already occupied. Clearly, despite the chain coffee shops in the high street, some people preferred a more intimate café. Or perhaps it was the fact that it sold books that attracted them here.

The bell made a muted sound as he opened the door. Clearly it was in need of attention. But Luke quickly found an empty table and subsided onto a chair. The smell of cakes and pastries was appetising, and, picking up the menu, he used it as a shield as he surveyed the interior of the café.

It was tastefully decorated, one wall covered with a mural of muffins and cupcakes that fairly oozed with fruit and cream you could almost taste. A huge Italian coffee machine bubbled away in the background, giving the place a contemporary feel, and away to the right an archway led into the bookshop.

'What can I get you?'

He'd been so intent on studying his surroundings, Luke hadn't heard anyone's approach. Putting the menu aside, he looked up at the young woman standing beside the table.

'Um—an Americano, please,' he was beginning, and then broke off in disbelief. 'Abby!' He got automatically to his feet. 'What the hell are you doing here?'

'I own the business,' Abby said, feeling amazingly calm.

She'd gone through the whole gamut of emotions in the last few weeks since she'd read the solicitor's letter, but at no time had she ever imagined that Luke might come into the café.

Alone.

She moistened her lips. 'I don't have to ask you why you're here, of course. I assume you're evaluating your latest acquisition.'

Luke stared down at her. He hadn't changed at all. Tall, dark-haired and olive-skinned, he was just as attractive as ever. Dangerously so, she acknowledged, wishing she were able to put the past behind her.

As he had evidently done.

She'd changed a lot, she was sure. An aborted love affair and a bitter divorce could do that to you. Not to mention discovering that what little money she'd invested in the café was now lost.

'You run this café?' he asked, as if he hadn't believed her the first time. 'I assumed you were still working in London. I had no idea you'd moved out of town.'

'Hadn't you?' Abby wondered if she believed him. If that were so, then the Morelli Corporation buying these shops was not the vindictive action on his part she'd thought it was.

'Of course, I hadn't,' muttered Luke, as if aware of her scepticism. 'I wouldn't have thought your husband would give up his job so easily. The stock market, wasn't it? Not much use for an investment broker around here.'

'Harry and I are divorced,' said Abby, aware that their prolonged conversation was attracting the attention of her other customers. 'I'll get your coffee.'

'Wait.' As she would have moved away, Luke's low voice arrested her. 'How long have you been divorced?'

'I don't think that's anything to do with you,' replied Abby, glad there was no tremor in her voice. 'Is that all?'

Luke scowled. 'Is this how you treat all your customers? Because if so—'

'You're not really a customer, Mr Morelli, are you? You're on a fact-finding mission. And I can always refuse to serve you. I have that right.'

Luke blew out a breath. He glanced about him, as if recognising there was no privacy here. 'Well, tell me a good place to eat and I'll buy you dinner this evening instead.'

'I don't think that's a good idea, Mr Morelli.' Abby refused to allow any trace of the temptation his words offered to show. With some relief she saw that two of her other customers had moved towards the till. 'I'll get your coffee.'

Luke had no choice but to let her go, and Abby hurried across to the counter. She had a few words with her departing regulars, rang up their tab, and then set about preparing the Americano Luke had asked for.

Her hands were shaking a little, but the machine did most of the work. She set his cup on a tray, added a small jug of cream and a sugar bowl containing both real and artificial sweeteners, and then turned back to deliver his coffee.

But Luke had gone. The table where he'd been sitting before their exchange was empty.

Setting the tray on the counter, she couldn't deny a sinking feeling in her stomach. Although she'd been shocked to see him, she'd never expected him to leave so precipitately.

So what? Did she want to see him again? After everything that had happened, was she fool enough to believe anything good could come of this encounter?

The day stretched endlessly ahead of her. It was an effort to think of anything but how unnerving it had been to see Luke again.

She'd thought about him many times, especially after her divorce was made final. But she'd known that, as far as he was concerned, she was still a liar and a cheat.

So why had he offered her dinner?

The café—and the bookshop—closed at four o'clock most days, and Abby wasn't usually eager to return to her flat upstairs where Harley was waiting for her.

Today, however, she couldn't wait to put on her coat, grab Harley's leash, and escape from the building. Luke's appearance had been a damning confirmation that his plans were going ahead.

Until then, she'd clung to the hope that they might not get planning permission, or they'd discover the ground was too damp for a development of that kind. But those hopes had now been shattered.

At the back of the row of shops, there was a stretch of open land, and Greg Hughes had said that that was another reason why Gifford's son was selling the properties. His father had owned the land, too, and, together with the shops that faced the street, the developers would have room for not only a car park, always useful in a town, but possibly a movie theatre, as well.

Still, for the moment, the land was unoccupied, and Harley really appreciated the opportunity to be let off the leash.

He wasn't a young dog, but he still had plenty of energy and Abby bent and picked up a twig and threw it across the grass.

Straight into the path of a man who was coming from the opposite direction.

Luke Morelli.

Abby reached the outer door and peered outside. Fortunately the floodlights were still on and she could see the dark green Aston Martin standing in a pool of light.

To her relief, its occupant didn't appear to have got out of the car. No doubt the rain—or perhaps the fact that he didn't know the address he wanted—was giving him pause.

Was it Luke Morelli? The rain made it difficult to see clearly. It certainly looked like him, so she had to take that chance. She couldn't allow her husband to come home and find him here.

She remembered too well the bruises on her breasts and stomach Harry had inflicted weeks ago when he'd discovered she'd had lunch with one of the professors from the university.

The fact that she could no longer wear her wedding ring, because he'd twisted her fingers so badly that the swelling was taking ages to go down, was another reason to turn on her. He was absurdly possessive. Particularly as God knew how many times he'd been unfaithful to her in the past.

Something she'd never even thought of.

Until now.

And she wasn't really interested in Luke Morelli, she insisted to herself as she ran across the gravel car park to where the car was waiting. He'd brought her home from the hen party a week ago. That was all. He hadn't even kissed her goodnight.

Although he'd wanted to. She was fairly sure of that. There'd been a moment, before she'd thrust open her door and hurriedly said good-night, when she'd thought he was going to lean across the console and touch her. And she'd wanted him to, she acknowledged. Just for a moment, she'd wanted to feel like a desirable woman again.

It was Luke, and without hesitation Abby pulled open the car door and got inside. 'You don't mind, do you?' she asked, indicating the rain. 'It's an awful night.'

'It just got a whole lot better,' said Luke with a grin. 'How did you know I was here?'

'Oh, you know...' Abby waved an airy hand. 'I was just looking out of the window, and I thought I recognised your car.'

'And you thought you'd come down and apologise for not ringing me,' suggested Luke drily. 'Do you have any idea how difficult it's been to find you?'

Abby's lips parted. 'You've been looking for me?' She hoped the alarm wasn't evident in her voice.

'Well, I've been trawling through the university webpages,' he admitted. 'But as I didn't know your surname or what the hell subject you were researching, I was just wasting my time.'

'Oh.' Abby's relief was almost palpable.

'So Ray, the guy I was with at the wine bar, suggested checking out your apartment.' He looked up at the apartment building. 'This is a classy place, isn't it?' His eyes darkened. 'I don't know whether I can afford you.'

'Oh—don't be silly. I—I share the apartment with—with a friend,' she stammered, not wanting him to think her job was anything special. 'Um—she's expecting me back. We were just going to have supper.' She reached for the door handle. 'I'm afraid I've got to go.'

Luke hesitated. 'You don't feel like going out for a meal instead?'

'I can't.' Abby knew she was tempting fate, even sitting here in Luke's car. 'I'm sorry. Some—some other time, perhaps.'

Now why had she said that?

'Okay.' Luke seized on the compromise. 'How about tomorrow night? I could pick you up here about eight. We could have dinner and then maybe a movie. What do you say?'

Abby hesitated. She knew she should refuse. For God's sake, if Harry even suspected she was considering going out with another man, she didn't like to think what he might do.

And some people might say that she'd deserve it, whatever it was. But heaven knew, she was desperate to spend an evening with someone who treated her with a little respect.

'I don't think so,' she said now, twisting her hands together in her lap. *'I—well, I don't know you.'*

'That can be arranged.'

'Can it?' God forgive her, she was actually considering it.

'So you do want to see me again?'

Abby hesitated once more. And this time, before she could even think of denying it, Luke looped a hand behind her head and brought her mouth to his.

'Let me persuade you,' he said huskily, and his tongue slipped silkily into her mouth.

Abby thought it was just as well she was sitting down at that moment. The hungry urgency of his kiss was robbing her of her sanity. Heat surrounded her, enveloping her in its sensual embrace. She found herself clutching the lapels of his leather jacket and arching towards him.

His mouth hardened, the kiss lengthening into a drugging seduction that showed no sign of ending. It was just as well the console was between them or she was fairly sure Luke would have hauled her onto his lap, and continued his sensual exploration below her waist.

As it was, he was cupping her breasts through the fine fabric of her velvet suit and she could feel her nipples peaking against his hands.

'Annabel, come with me,' he said roughly, lift-

ing the hem of her top to find the warm flesh of her midriff. And Abby was sorely tempted to give in.

And then another car accelerated into the lot and Abby's blood ran cold. She'd recognised that car over Luke's shoulder, and it was as she had anticipated upstairs: Harry had come home earlier than he'd said.

Dragging her mouth away from Luke's, she reached again for the handle of the door. 'I—I can't. I've got to go. H-Harriet's waiting for me.'

'Wait!' Before she could get the door open, Luke had grabbed her arm. 'At least agree to go out with me tomorrow evening,' he said. 'What's your name? I don't even know your surname. Let me give you a ring. What's your number?'

'No.' Abby wasn't that crazy. 'I—I'll ring you.'

'When?'

Abby could see Harry parking his car now and panic made her reckless. 'Tomorrow,' she said. 'I'll ring you tomorrow.'

'You promise?'

'I promise,' she said, aware that she was feeling breathless. 'Please, I have to go now.'

'Okay. But take my card.'

He handed it to her as he released her, and she stuffed it into her pocket before scrambling *out of the car and running quickly across the car park to the apartment building.*

Hopefully, Luke would put her haste down to the rain, Abby thought as she ducked into the lift, grateful that the doorman was still ensconced in front of his TV. And with a bit of luck, Harry wouldn't even notice that she'd left the apartment.

Luke's phone rang late in the evening. He'd been reading some official documents prior to a meeting the following day and the unexpected sound brought a scowl to his face.

He was inclined not to answer it. The girl he'd been seeing in recent weeks wouldn't take no for an answer, and he couldn't think of anyone else who might ring him after eleven o'clock.

The screen indicated that it was an unknown caller, and it could be his father. He hadn't seen Oliver Morelli for weeks. Still, unless there was some emergency, even he was unlikely to ring at this time.

Cursing himself for being a fool, Luke picked the phone up from his desk and accepted the call.

'Luke?'

Luke blew out a startled breath. If he wasn't mistaken, it was Annabel, the girl who'd said she would ring him three weeks ago and who hadn't kept her promise.

Until now.

'Annabel?' he said warily, wondering if he was so pleased to hear from her that he was mistaking someone else's voice for hers. 'It is Annabel, isn't it?'

She gave a nervous laugh. 'You've forgotten me so soon?'

'No.' Luke ran his tongue over his dry lips. 'I was beginning to think you'd forgotten me.'

'Not likely,' she said, but there was a distinctly nervous tremor in her voice. 'How are you?'

'I'm fine.' Luke hesitated. 'But it's a little late to be making a social call, isn't it?'

'I'm sorry.'

He was afraid she was going to ring off, and he continued hurriedly, 'But I am glad to hear from you.' He paused. 'Does this mean you'll agree to a date?'

'Sort of.' He heard her blow out a breath. 'What are you doing right now?'

'Right now?' Luke was taken aback. 'I'm working. How about you?'

'Oh...' She hesitated. 'I've not been doing much.' Another pause. 'I wondered if you'd like to go for a drink.'

Luke almost gasped. 'Now?'

'If you'd like to.'

But it's so late, was on the tip of Luke's tongue, and he had to bite it back. 'Um—I guess so,' he said instead, wondering what the hell he was letting himself in for. 'Do you want me to pick you up?'

'No.' Her response was immediate. 'I'll meet you.'

'Where?'

'I—how about the Parker House? We both know where that is.'

'O-kay.' Luke dragged the word out. 'If you're sure you don't want a lift.'

'I'm sure,' she said. 'In about half an hour, yes?'

Luke shook his head perplexedly. 'I'll be there.'

Deciding the black sweater and matching jeans he was wearing would do for the Parker House, Luke grabbed his leather jacket and stowed his wallet and his phone in his pockets.

Outside, it was cold, but at least it was fine, a three-quarters moon adding its silvery light to the dark streets. Luke lived in north London and at this time of night he had little difficulty driving into the West End.

But his mind was buzzing with questions. What in God's name was Annabel doing, phoning him at this time of night and suggesting they should meet for a drink? Had she been drinking already? She hadn't struck him as the kind of girl to go on a binge, but who knew?

He managed to park in a side road not far from his destination and he strode quickly along the street towards the wine bar. There were quite a few people in the vicinity, some of them just hanging about outside.

Having no idea where Annabel wanted to meet, Luke entered the wine bar, scanning the busy bar area for any sign of her. It didn't look as if she was here yet, and he stopped at the bar and ordered a beer.

'Hi.'

The voice came from close by and he turned to find Annabel hovering behind him. She looked as lovely as ever, but paler than he remembered. She was wearing a black coat, the collar tipped up around her ears, and her hair was in an untidy knot on top of her head. She was wearing very little make-up, and Luke wondered again what she'd been doing before she made that call.

'Hi,' he said, relieved at least to see she'd made it okay. 'What would you like to drink?'

'Oh—do you think we could go somewhere else?' she asked, glancing behind her. 'This place is awfully noisy, don't you think?'

It was, but Luke was tempted to ask why she'd

asked him to meet her here if she didn't like it. So, 'Where?' he asked, paying the bartender for the bottle of beer he'd been handed. 'It's going to be noisy everywhere at this time of night.' He paused. 'Look, there's an empty booth over there. Why don't we sit down and talk about it?'

She shrugged, but he could tell she wasn't happy. Still, she agreed to the glass of wine he suggested, and Luke commandeered the booth before anyone else could take it.

'That's better,' he said, sliding onto the banquette beside her. His hip nudged hers and he thought she caught her breath.

She smelled incredible, a sensual, exotic scent that filled his nostrils and fired his blood. God, he wanted her, he thought unsteadily. What were the chances of him persuading her to come back to his apartment?

'Why don't you take off your coat?' he suggested. 'It's warm in here.'

'Oh, I...' If anything, she wrapped the collar of the coat more closely about her, and Luke sighed.

'It doesn't matter what you're wearing, you know,' he told her gently, bending to nuzzle his face against her soft cheek. 'I can't tell you how good it is to see you again. I was seriously thinking you'd decided to write me off.'

Annabel gave a husky laugh. 'I wouldn't do that.'

'So—what? You'd let me know if I was wasting my time, right? Because I have to tell you, Annabel, I don't think I've ever felt like this before.'

'You don't mean that.'

'I do.' Luke cupped her chin in his hand and turned her face to his. 'I'm not saying I've led a monk-like existence. What man has?' He brushed her lips with his. 'But this is different. You're different.' He kissed her again, more thoroughly this time. 'How would you feel if I asked you to come back to my apartment?'

Annabel caught her breath. 'Your apartment?' she breathed, drawing back when he would have kissed her again, and as she did so the collar of her coat fell away, revealing an ugly bruise on her neck. 'Where do you live?'

'North London. Camden.' But Luke was more interested in how she'd got that bruise on her neck. Although she drew back, he touched it with gentle fingers. 'How did this happen?'

'Oh...' She pulled her collar up again, and shook her head. 'I fell. In the bathroom. Stupid, huh?' She changed the subject. 'Do you live alone?'

'Well, I don't have a partner, if that's what you're asking,' he said humorously. 'Do you?'

'*Funny you should ask that.*'

Two things happened in quick succession: the man who had spoken, a man Luke had never seen before, slid into the booth opposite them; and Annabel said, '*Harry!*' in a shocked voice, and shifted away from Luke, proving she did know who the newcomer was.

He was a heavy man, not particularly tall, but broad and muscular, with the kind of self-satisfied confidence Luke encountered in the boardrooms of the companies he dealt with every day.

If he had to guess, and judging by the cut of the suit the guy was wearing, Luke would say he probably worked in the City. So who was he? Annabel's boyfriend? Her partner? Surely not.

The guy cast Luke a contemptuous look. '*Aren't you going to introduce me to your companion, Abby?*'

Abby?

Luke remembered his earlier suspicion that that might be her name.

Abby shifted a little nervously. '*Um—this is Luke. Luke Morelli,*' she said, her voice barely audible. '*He's—he's just a friend.*'

'*With benefits, if I'm any judge,*' said Harry, his eyes not leaving Abby's face. '*Isn't it lucky that I decided to come looking for you here?*'

Abby took a steadying breath, or that was

how it seemed to Luke, and seemed to gain some resolution. 'You said you wouldn't be back until tomorrow,' she exclaimed accusingly.

'And you said you were going to have an early night.' Harry arched a mocking brow. 'What a lying little bitch you are!'

'Take that back!'

Slamming his hands down on the table, Luke got to his feet and reached for the other man's collar. Hauling him up out of his seat, he said savagely, 'Who the hell do you think you are, speaking to her like that? I've a good mind to...'

'No, Luke!'

Abby was on her feet now, reaching for his arm as he was thinking of ramming his fist into the other man's face. And Harry, if that was his name, gave a harsh laugh.

'Listen to her, Luke,' he said, raising a hand to his throat and easing himself away. 'Ask her what gives me the right to expect a certain measure of loyalty from her. I bet she hasn't mentioned me, has she?'

Luke scowled. 'Well, if you're her boyfriend, you should show her more respect,' he said harshly. He turned to Annabel—Abby—and waited for her to speak. 'Who is this loser? Do you know him?'

Which even he knew was a stupid question in the circumstances. But, Goddammit, he felt as if he'd suddenly stepped into an alternative universe.

It was the man who answered, his expression as smug as the words he uttered.

'She's my wife, Luke. Has been for—let me see—three years. And if she wants a divorce, she only has to ask for one. Isn't that right, Abby? Go on, Luke, ask her if she wants a divorce. But I think you'll find she doesn't. My wife has expensive tastes that I doubt you could satisfy. What do you say, Abby? Tell your—friend—that I'm right.'

Abby didn't answer him and Luke felt the bottom drop out of his world. But he wouldn't ask her if she wanted a divorce. It was obvious, he'd been a fool to believe her. She had no intention of leaving her husband. She'd played them both for fools.

CHAPTER THREE

HARLEY SAW THE man coming towards them and raced excitedly towards him. Clearly, Luke didn't inspire the same reaction in him as Greg Hughes. Considering the muddy ground, Abby hoped Luke wasn't thinking of suing her for a new suit.

Harley's paws could be lethal.

The dog fussed about the man, wagging his tail. Oh, Harley, you Judas, Abby intoned silently as Luke bent to scratch the retriever's head.

She'd thought he might not have heard her approach, but, as if on cue, Luke straightened to face her. 'Your dog?' he asked as Harley bounded back to his mistress, and Abby nodded.

'Mine,' she agreed, half wishing she'd chosen another route for their walk.

'He's a beautiful animal.' Luke came closer as she struggled to find the clasp of the leash. 'Hey, don't bother fastening him up on my account. I like dogs, and fortunately they usually like me.'

Why was she not surprised? Finding the catch, she fastened the leash to Harley's collar, anyway. He whined a little plaintively, but she refused to be deterred. 'I didn't think anyone else was about or I wouldn't have let him run free.'

Luke shrugged, glancing about him. 'I was just familiarising myself with the area. It's a beautiful part of the country.'

'It is.' What else could she say? That was why she'd moved here, for heaven's sake. 'Do you know it well?'

Luke shrugged again. 'My father lives in Bath these days, but I don't know Ashford-St-James very well.'

So how on earth had he found out about the properties? wondered Abby curiously. Or had he been searching the Internet and come upon them, much as she'd done herself four years ago?

As if reading her thoughts, he said, 'It was my father who alerted me to the sale. He used to play golf with Charles Gifford, the father of the present owner.'

'Yes. I know who Charles Gifford is—*was*,' said Abby flatly.

'So I guess you knew that I was involved before I walked into the café a few hours ago?'

Abby nodded. 'I got a letter, the same as everybody else.'

'And you've been cursing me ever since,' remarked Luke cynically. 'Don't look like that. I can tell.'

Abby sighed. 'As a matter of fact, my first thought was that you knew I owned one of the businesses, and you'd bought them as—as a kind of revenge,' she said honestly.

Luke snorted. 'You're kidding me.'

'No.' Abby was defensive. 'We didn't exactly part on the best of terms, did we?'

'No.' Luke conceded the point. 'But you must have quite an opinion of yourself if you think I'm still stressing over something that happened, what? Four years ago?'

'Five,' said Abby shortly, wondering if he'd really forgotten. 'Anyway, I'm glad I left no lasting scar on your life.'

If she only knew, thought Luke grimly, looking down at the retriever again so she wouldn't see the hostility in his eyes.

She'd only been responsible for his break-up with Ray Carpenter, who hadn't been able to stand the bitter way Luke had come to regard his life.

And she'd also been the reason he'd married Sonia, the girl he'd been seeing in the weeks before Annabel—*Abby*—had come on the scene. The marriage had been a mistake from the outset and a year later, it had been over.

Now he made a dismissive gesture, amazed the lie came so easily. 'I'd forgotten all about it,' he said carelessly. 'Like you, I've moved on with my life.'

'Well, I'm glad.' Abby gazed up at him, rather guiltily, he thought. 'It was all my fault that—well, what happened, happened,' she said.

That had been Luke's take on it certainly. Nothing could alter the fact that she'd been married when she'd agreed to meet him. He should have felt sorry for her husband, instead of threatening to sock him on the jaw.

He knew he shouldn't be having this conversation with her. As soon as he'd walked into the café and discovered who the owner of the business was, he should have left it there. Instead, he'd spent the last few hours hanging around Ashford, trying to think of a reason to go back.

When she'd come to serve him, he'd been staggered—and angered—by his reaction. He'd had no idea she'd moved to the town and opened a café. She'd been a researcher in English at the university. An academic. As soon as he'd learned her real name from Harry, it had been easy enough to find out where she worked.

He'd also discovered that her husband—

Harry Laurence—had worked in the city. He was fairly well-known in stockbroking circles, although some people considered he was a bit of a barbarian.

Luke had wondered if the bruise he'd seen on Abby's neck that night had been put there by her husband. But then he remembered Harry's boast that she would never leave him.

And she hadn't.

She could have got a divorce. If she'd had any self-respect, she would have. Luke knew from his own unhappy experience, divorces were not that hard to come by.

He wondered when she had got a divorce, and whether she'd been the one to initiate it. Recalling how she'd deceived her husband, Luke thought it was reasonable to assume he'd been the one who had finally wanted out.

Even so, he hadn't forgotten a moment of their time together. He could still taste her sweetness on his tongue. An affair that had never become an affair, he reminded himself bitterly. She'd left the wine bar with her husband, and, until today, he'd never seen her again.

It didn't please him that she was even more attractive now than she'd been five years ago. And oh, yes, he knew exactly how long it was since that scene at the Parker House.

His presumed stumble over the years had

been a deliberate attempt to disconcert her. Unfortunately, it had had the opposite effect.

Had she gained a little weight? If so, it suited her. And her hair wasn't as ghostly pale as it had been before. It was still thick, and a rich honey blonde, with silver highlights. But she'd drawn it back into a ponytail, exposing the delicate bones of her face.

So why was he noticing these things? Did he want to risk her making a fool of him again? He still wanted to have sex with her. That much was unfortunately true. But it was just a physical thing and he had no intention of acting on it.

She seemed to hesitate, and then said, 'You left without your coffee this morning.' A faint smile touched her lips. 'Were you afraid I might poison it?'

Luke's lips tightened. 'No, I can honestly say, that didn't occur to me.' Probably because he considered she was too clever to make a mistake like that, however much she might resent him.

'Good.' She caught her lower lip between her teeth. 'I shouldn't like there to be any animosity between us.'

'Us?' Luke scowled. 'There is no "us".'

Faint colour touched her cheeks. 'Not now. I know that.'

'Not ever,' he interrupted her harshly.

'Okay.' She paused, and then said hurriedly,

'I hope you don't think I'm trying to use our past—association—to influence you in your decision about—about the development.'

'Oh, please.' He held up a hand. 'You couldn't.' He paused. 'And I'd rather not be reminded that I was almost responsible for you cheating on your husband. Or maybe that wasn't the first time.'

Abby was furious. 'If you remember, it wasn't me who started it. You were on the lookout for a casual hook-up and I was there.'

'That's not true!'

'Isn't it?' Her lips twisted. 'I bet you thought you were onto a good thing.'

'Well, I got that wrong, didn't I?' he snarled, and she shook her head disbelievingly.

'I can't believe you said that,' she exclaimed. 'How could I ever have been attracted to you?'

'Abby...'

To his frustration, the retriever chose that moment to wind itself about his legs, throwing him off balance. Without thinking, he tried to save himself by clutching her shoulder, and Abby's arm curled automatically about his waist.

The atmosphere was suddenly charged with tension. Luke was overwhelmingly conscious of Abby's warm body close against his own. It was not a situation he'd engineered, but now that it had happened, he was unwillingly—and undeniably—aroused.

Stifling a groan of anguish, he grabbed the leash and set himself free. 'I think I should go.'

'Yes, I think you should,' she said tightly. 'But don't leave on my account. I'm going back to Harley's myself.'

For a moment, his mind was too caught up with other things. Primarily what he'd like to do to her body. Then he realised what she'd meant. 'Oh, the café?' he said flatly, and she nodded.

Then, almost against her better judgement, she said, 'Please don't penalise any of the other tenants because of me.'

'I don't see how I could do that.'

'Oh, don't underestimate yourself, Luke.' Abby spoke bitterly. 'This isn't an easy situation for any of us.'

'I'm sorry.'

'Are you?' She didn't sound as if she believed him. 'Well, if you'll excuse me...'

Luke groaned. 'What do you expect from me, Abby? Absolution?'

'You're joking!' She held up her head. 'I expect nothing from you, Luke. I never did.'

Luke's jaw hardened. 'That wasn't my impression. But, perhaps, I was wrong. I was wrong about so much else about you, wasn't I?'

'You arrogant bastard!'

Abby grasped Harley's leash in both hands and backed away from him. Her features were pale now and taut with outrage, and Luke knew a feeling of grim frustration. He hadn't intended to hurt her, but he evidently had, and, unable to do anything else, he went after her.

'Abby…'

'Stay away from me!'

'I don't want to fight with you.' He sounded as if he regretted what he'd said, and he didn't like it.

'Don't you?' he thought she muttered as she turned away from him and started back towards the road. 'Well, don't worry,' she called back over her shoulder. 'I'll pretend this conversation never happened. Just get your solicitor to let me know when you want the café vacating, and I'll be out of there.'

With a feeling of defeat, Luke strode after her, grasping her arm and swinging her round to face him. There were tears staining her cheeks, he saw at once, and, unable to prevent himself, he lifted a hand and used his thumb to brush them away.

'Don't,' she whispered, but he wasn't listening to her. His mind was filled with images of the hot, steamy sex they might have shared if things had been different, and it was difficult to remember exactly why he shouldn't be touching her.

Her cheek was so soft beneath his fingers, and he allowed his hand to move lower until his thumb was stroking the parted contours of her mouth.

She didn't try to stop him. She was still gripping the retriever's leash like a lifeline, but Luke was intoxicated by her scent. Unable to prevent himself, he bent towards her and covered her lips with his.

Her mouth was hot and unexpectedly vulnerable, and all the emotions she'd aroused in him five years ago came flooding back.

He knew instantly why he hadn't forgotten her, why he could remember so well her taste and her smell. And the sensual pressure of her hips against his erection made sanity desert him.

'Luke…'

His name was barely audible. Her breath hitched, and her hand curling around his neck was so cold it burned him. Or perhaps it was his skin that was burning up with the sudden intensity of his desire.

One thing was certain: he couldn't let this go on. He knew that this stretch of open ground, despite supporting a few trees, was hardly private. And, unfortunately, they were not hidden by any of those trees.

Apart from which, what in God's name did he think he was doing?

And then Harley barked, bringing an abrupt end to his uncertainty.

Maybe the retriever had seen a cat or a rabbit. He'd started tugging on his leash, and Abby was forced to take an involuntary step away from Luke.

'Harley,' she exclaimed, and Luke expelled a hoarse breath.

Dammit, he'd never thought he'd be grateful to a dog, but he was.

'I've got to go,' he said roughly as Abby endeavoured to calm the animal down.

And without giving her time to say anything else, he strode away.

CHAPTER FOUR

A WEEK LATER, Abby had succeeded in putting what she preferred to call 'Luke's uncalled-for assault' out of her mind.

It had been an aberration, nothing more. On his part, and probably on hers, as well. For God's sake, she'd thought she'd got what had happened five years ago into perspective. She was a free, independent woman these days; not the pathetic abused wife she used to be.

It was late afternoon, and Lori had already gone to collect her daughter from school, and, as there were no customers, Abby decided to close up a little earlier than usual.

It had been a dank afternoon, and frankly few people had been about. When the door opened, she thought her assistant must have forgotten something and had come back to collect it. But, instead, it was Greg Hughes.

Her heart sank. She so wasn't in the mood to talk to the photographer and, not for the first time, she wished she didn't live over the café and could say she was on her way home.

She'd just finished cleaning the coffee machine when he strolled over with a proprietorial air to rest his elbows on the polished counter.

'You heard anything yet?' he asked rudely, without offering a greeting, and Abby turned from her task to give him a cool stare.

'I beg your pardon?'

'I said…'

'Yes, I heard what you said.' Abby regarded him with cold inquiry. 'I just don't know what you're talking about.'

Greg scowled. 'The development,' he said impatiently. 'Have you heard any more about the development?' He paused. 'I assume you've read your letter by now.'

'Oh.' The development and the *developer* were the last things she wanted to think about. 'Then, yes, I've read the solicitor's letter, and no, I haven't heard anything else.'

Greg sniffed. 'Well, it's a rum affair, if you ask me,' he said. 'I want to know what kind of compensation they're offering.'

'Compensation?'

'Yes. They've got to pay me something for the eighteen months that are left on my lease. Until they do, I won't know what kind of replacement premises I'll be able to afford.'

'I see.'

''Course, you won't have that problem, will you?' he went on smugly. 'By the time you get your marching orders, your lease will have run out.'

'How do you know that?'

'You told me you only had six months left.' Greg was unrepentant. 'I just wondered, as you seemed to know the guy, if he'd given you a heads-up.'

Abby was tempted to lie and say she didn't know Luke. But she couldn't be sure that someone hadn't seen them last week on the waste ground behind the shops.

'I think I said I knew *of* his company,' she said, hiding her crossed fingers. 'I—well, I believe he was round here the other day, checking out his investment. Anonymously, apparently.'

'Really?' Clearly Greg hadn't heard anything about this, and Abby realised belatedly that she'd virtually admitted recognising Luke.

But Greg didn't pick her up on it, evidently assuming someone else had told her the news. 'Well, well,' he said. 'I wish I'd seen Morelli. I'd have felt like giving him a piece of my mind.'

'Would you? That's interesting.'

Abby started in surprise. She'd been so intent on not giving Greg any reason to suspect she knew more than she was saying that she hadn't heard the door open. Which wasn't surprising because the bell was definitely on its last legs.

Greg started, too, eyes turning apprehensively to look over his shoulder. But, he didn't recognise the newcomer and a certain look of belligerence crossed his face.

'Do you mind?' he said, before Abby could say anything. 'This is a private conversation.'

'Oh, I'm sorry.' Luke closed the door and crossed the café with lithe, easy grace. 'I thought I heard my name mentioned. Something about giving me a piece of your mind, wasn't it?'

Greg's jaw dropped. 'You're Morelli?' he exclaimed disbelievingly, and Abby couldn't say she was surprised.

In jeans and a navy turtleneck, a leather jacket looking distinctly as if it had seen better days, Luke looked nothing like the successful entrepreneur she knew him to be.

Evidently, Greg was taken aback, as much by Luke's appearance as by what he'd said. He turned back to Abby, raising his eyebrows in stunned inquiry, and she made an involuntary movement of her shoulders that she hoped Luke hadn't seen.

'So...?' Luke joined Greg at the counter. 'Do you want to tell me who you are? I don't believe I caught your name.'

'It's Hughes. Greg Hughes,' the man muttered unwillingly. 'I own the photography studio next door.'

'I see.' Luke nodded. 'So, Mr Hughes, what did you want to say to me? I'm listening.'

Greg's jaw jutted defensively. Then, as if realising he had to say something, he said, 'I just don't agree with—with people—'

'Like myself,' put in Luke helpfully, and Abby sensed he was enjoying this.

'Well, yeah.' Greg sniffed. 'I don't think you realise how old this parade of shops is.' And when Luke didn't answer, 'And you're just going to pull them all down and put up a supermarket. It's sacrilege, that's what it is. Sacrilege!'

Abby saw Luke give her an inquiring look. 'Is this your opinion, as well, Mrs Laurence?'

Abby flushed. 'It's *Ms* Lacey,' she said, aware, with some irritation, that Greg was regarding her curiously now. 'I—well, I resumed my maiden name after—after buying the business.'

'Ah.'

Luke's dark eyes assessed her with disturbing intensity, and she was instantly aware that the ponytail, with which she'd started the day, was now shedding strands of damp hair onto her shoulders. She also still had on the apron she'd worn to clean the equipment, and she was sure it looked definitely the worse for wear.

Dammit!

'But you didn't answer my question—Ms Lacey.'

Luke was speaking again, but before she could respond Greg answered for her.

'Of course she agrees with me,' he exclaimed belligerently. 'How do you think we all feel? This is our livelihood. And in Abby's case, her home, as well.'

'Really?' Abby saw Luke absorb this piece of information and could have slapped Greg for giving out her personal details to a man she'd hoped never to see again.

'Yes, really,' Greg continued, apparently unaware of—or indifferent to—Abby's feelings. 'At least I had the sense to buy another house while property was cheap.'

'I'm sure Mr Morelli isn't interested in our problems, Greg,' Abby inserted, glaring at him. She straightened her spine. 'What can I do for you, Mr Morelli? Or did you just come here to sample my coffee?'

'Hey, that's a good idea,' broke in Greg again, much to her frustration. 'And you should try one of Abby's blueberry muffins. If they don't persuade you to think again about the development, nothing will.'

'Greg!' Abby was horrified. The last thing she wanted was for Luke to think that she and

Greg Hughes had been conspiring against him. 'I don't think anything we say—or do—will change Mr Morelli's mind.'

Luke crossed his arms, tucking his hands beneath his armpits. He was tempted to say 'You got that right', but, despite his feelings towards Abby, he was loath to embarrass her in front of this oaf.

'Perhaps I will have a coffee, after all,' he said, aware that his words were probably just as irritating to Abby's ears as what Hughes had said had been. 'If it's not too much trouble.'

He saw Abby's lips tighten. 'I'm afraid that's not possible, Mr Morelli,' she said stiffly. 'I've just closed the machine down for the night.'

Greg Hughes snorted. 'Looks like you're out of luck, Morelli,' he said, not without a certain amount of satisfaction. He paused. 'I guess you'll just have to tell us what you're doing here without one of the perks of the job.'

Luke's eyes narrowed. 'I don't believe I invited you to hear what I had to say to Ms Lacey,' he remarked neutrally. 'I'm sure you've got better things to do than stand around here talking to me.'

The photographer scowled. Then he looked at Abby. 'Do you want me to go, Abby?' he asked pointedly. 'I can stick around for a bit, if you'd rather.'

Luke could tell Abby had mixed feelings. He sensed she was no friend of the photographer, but then she was no friend of Luke's either.

'That's okay, Greg,' she said after a moment. 'I'm good. I'll let you know later if Mr Morelli has any news.'

She was anything but good, thought Luke grimly, as, with some reluctance, Greg Hughes let himself out of the café. And now they were alone, she was evidently eager for him to be gone, too.

As soon as the door had closed, she said, 'I was of the opinion we had nothing more to say to one another, Mr Morelli. And as I was about to close the café, I'd be grateful if you could get to the point of this visit.'

In truth, Luke wasn't absolutely sure what the point of his visit was. Okay, his father had phoned and said he'd got a touch of flu, but that wouldn't normally have been reason enough for Luke to abandon any meetings he'd had arranged and drive down to Bath to see him.

In fact, before he'd heard from his father, he'd seriously been considering taking a break from business and asking the young woman he was presently seeing whether she fancied a trip to the Seychelles. Blue skies, blue water, tropical breezes, and five-star accommodation sounded pretty good to him, and he guessed it would sound pretty good to Jodi, too.

So why was he here in Ashford-St-James, lying to his father about checking out building regulations, to cross swords with a woman he'd sworn had nearly ruined his life? He was over her now, wasn't he? Except for that niggling feeling of unfinished business where she was concerned.

'Okay,' he said, after a moment, 'why don't you tell me why you chose to leave a perfectly good job in London to move down here?'

Abby's jaw dropped. 'You're not serious.'

'Humour me.'

'Why should I? What I do—or did—is nothing to do with you.'

Luke sighed. 'I'd like to know. What happened to make you change your life so drastically?'

Abby shook her head. He thought she wasn't going to answer him. Then she said flatly, 'I got a divorce. That's what happened. But you know that. So why are you asking these questions?'

Luke frowned. 'I guess I'm wondering whether, after losing this business, you'll be moving back to London.'

Abby stared at him for a moment without speaking. Then she turned and bent to deposit the cloth she'd been using below the counter.

'I think you'd better go, Mr Morelli,' she said. 'I have no intention of answering any more of your questions.'

Luke watched her remove her apron and stow it in what appeared to be a laundry basket at the back of the serving area. Then she smoothed her hands down over what he could now see was a short pleated skirt above those long, spectacular legs.

If she was aware that he was watching her, she ignored it. She came to the end of the counter, and regarded him without a shred of liking in her cool gaze.

'Please go,' she said tersely. 'I want to lock up.'

Luke's hands dropped to his sides and he shoved his fingers into the back pockets of his jeans. Doing so tightened the fabric across his abdomen and he was instantly conscious of his semi-erection. His zip pressed uncomfortably against his groin and he was glad she was so intent on getting rid of him that she didn't pay him any attention.

But he had one more parting shot. 'I guess,' he said provocatively as he strolled towards the outer door, 'when Laurence threw you out, it would have been difficult to maintain your standard of living in the city. I hope he's paying you some alimony. Losing this place will be quite a blow.'

He felt rather than saw her brush past him. Yanking open the door ahead of him, she said angrily, 'Get out!'

Luke was in no hurry. 'The truth hurts, doesn't it?' he remarked mockingly. 'You should have considered the consequences before you thought of breaking your marriage vows.'

He was almost sure there were tears in her eyes now, but he refused to show her any remorse. It was time she started paying for what she'd done.

But as he stepped out into the street, he had to admit he didn't feel the sense of closure he'd expected. It would come, though, he assured himself. Just as soon as he demolished the café and all the other businesses on this row.

But as the door slammed behind him he wished he didn't feel such a bastard.

CHAPTER FIVE

LUKE'S PLANE LANDED at Heathrow just after eight a.m.

His flight had been delayed in Hong Kong, and he'd had to kick his heels around the international airport there for more than three hours.

By the time he got out of the arrivals lounge at Heathrow and found his chauffeur, Felix, waiting for him, he was in no mood to make nice with anyone.

'Good trip?' queried Felix, getting behind the wheel, and Luke gave him a dour look.

'How long have you been waiting?' he asked, instead of answering the man, and Felix shrugged.

'A couple of hours, give or take,' he said pleasantly. 'I checked the flight online and saw there'd been a delay. But I never trust those schedules. I prefer to come to the airport and see for myself.'

That, at least, drew a rueful smile from his employer.

'They're usually reliable, you know,' Luke said drily. Then, hooking one ankle across his knee, he gazed out of the car's windows at the overcast sky. 'It's been a long journey.'

'I'll bet.' Felix glanced at him through the rear-view mirror. 'Maybe you should have gone to Mahe, after all.'

'Yeah.'

Luke conceded the point, but said nothing more. Maybe he should have taken Jodi to the Seychelles as he'd originally intended. But after that trip to Ashford-St-James, he'd been in no mood to spend time with another woman.

Instead, he'd spent a couple of weeks in Melbourne, catching up with what Ray Carpenter and his family were doing. And avoiding thinking about the development he'd been planning before he went away.

'So,' he said resignedly, 'is there any news?'

'I suppose it depends what you mean by news,' replied Felix evenly. 'Some guy involved with that site you're hoping to develop in Wiltshire has started a petition. He's claiming that the buildings you're thinking of demolishing have historical significance and should be placed under a preservation order.'

Luke didn't ask how the man had got his information. Somehow Felix always knew what was going on. But he didn't have to think very hard to guess who he was talking about.

Greg Hughes!

So was Abby involved? He would have to find out.

It was almost dark when Abby got home after walking Harley. And raining quite heavily, too.

They'd circled the park a couple of times and then Abby had called at the local deli for groceries. She didn't like to admit it, but it was true: Ashford-St-James did need a decent supermarket. One with its own parking area. That was one disadvantage about the café. There was nowhere to park nearby.

Not that she owned a car, she reflected with a sigh. She owned an old van that she used to collect supplies from the wholesalers, but that was all. And that had to be parked in the alley between the row of shops.

Her divorce from Harry had not been a pretty one, and, after paying for her mother's funeral, Abby had been virtually broke. Only the modest price she'd got for her mother's terraced house had enabled her to move away from London. But she'd been so desperate to escape, she'd have sacrificed any amount of money to be free.

She tried not to think about it these days.

Leaving London had been the best thing she could have done. Had she stayed in the capital, she knew Harry would have found some way to hurt her. He was a vindictive man, and only the fear that his friends would make fun of him if he contested the divorce had forced him to let her go.

Abby let herself into the side door of the café premises and, after locking it and setting the dead bolt, she climbed the stairs to her apartment.

Harley frolicked ahead of her, full of beans after his walk. But Abby took the stairs a little more slowly, wondering how much longer she would be allowed to stay here.

It was a Friday evening, but, from her point of view, the weekend was usually her busiest time. Shoppers, who came into the small town at weekends to do their weekly shop, often came into the café for either coffee or lunch. But at least she'd have a whole day off on Sunday.

Inside the apartment, she went into the small kitchen to put her shopping away and give Harley his supper. As well as the kitchen, there was a living room, which she'd furnished from the saleroom, with a dining alcove, and a reasonably-sized bedroom and bath. It was nothing like the upmarket apartment she'd shared with Harry. But, by comparison, it was heaven on earth.

Or it had been.

With the retriever seen to, Abby regarded the contents of her fridge without enthusiasm. She wasn't particularly hungry and she decided to have a shower before tackling her own meal.

Leaving Harley to his kibble, she went into the bedroom, kicking off her shoes as she did so. The shower was hot and she stood for several minutes letting the water cascade over her. She usually enjoyed the sensation, but tonight she couldn't seem to relax.

She hadn't forgotten that it was over three weeks since Luke's visit to the café. Three weeks since they'd had that altercation that had culminated in Abby throwing him out. Well, asking him to go, she amended ruefully. There was no way she could have got him to leave if he hadn't decided to do so.

Whatever, she knew he was the real cause of her depression. And not just because of the business either. It was obvious he still considered that she was to blame for Harry's behaviour. But she was damned if she was going to try and tell him the truth, only to have him throw her words back in her face.

Besides, since moving to Ashford, she'd put all that misery behind her. Just occasionally, when she went back to visit her mother's grave, the whole sorry affair jumped back into her mind.

Her mother would have been horrified had she even suspected the kind of life Abby had been leading before she died. But it had been worth it to ensure that Annabel Lacey had never wanted for anything.

Stepping out of the shower, she was towelling herself dry when she heard someone knocking at the outer door. Not to say 'hammering', she thought impatiently as Harley started barking. She wondered who on earth it could be.

The only person who came to mind was Greg Hughes and she had no intention of letting him in. But in all the years she'd been here, he'd never bothered her after dark.

The hammering started again and Harley's barking grew to a crescendo. If she wasn't careful, Miss Miller, who ran the gift shop on the other side of the café, and who also lived above the business, would begin to think something was wrong.

She couldn't have that, and, tossing the towel aside, she wrung most of the water out of her hair and reached for her towelling bathrobe. Then, wrapping the folds about herself, she emerged into the living room where Harley was making so much noise.

'Quiet,' she said reprovingly, when the dog came to fuss about her. He was wagging his tail, but she knew better than to trust his judgement of who it might be.

It crossed her mind she shouldn't open the door without first identifying her caller. She had one or two friends in Ashford; Lori Yates, for instance. But she would usually ring before turning up.

Biting her tongue, she opened the door to the stairs and paused, switching on the light. Of course, Harley had no such reservations and immediately ran down the stairs to the hall below. He barked again, as if saying, *What are you waiting for?* And with a resigned sigh, Abby followed him down.

She hesitated and then called warily, 'Who is it?'

'Me!' Despite the fact that she shouldn't instantly recognise the voice, it was unmistakeable. 'Open the door, Abby. It's pouring down out here.'

Luke!

Abby expelled an unsteady breath. What was Luke doing at her door?

'I—I'm not dressed,' she replied at last as Harley started barking again. 'What do you want?'

Luke stifled an oath. 'Open the damn door,

Abby,' he exclaimed, his patience obviously shredding. 'Do you want me to get pneumonia?'

Abby was tempted to say she didn't care, one way or the other, but that wouldn't be true. She waited only another moment before releasing the bolt and pulling the heavy door open.

He was right. It was pouring, much worse now than it had been when they got back from their walk. A regular cloudburst had created a flood in the alley. Luke himself was soaked; the fabric of his jacket, which she suspected was cashmere, had darkened from silver grey to charcoal with the rain.

She bent and grabbed Harley and then stepped back automatically, and Luke dashed inside, closing the door behind him. A cool draught preceded him, making her shudder. Then he leaned back against the panels and regarded her between narrowed lids.

Abby knew his intent gaze was taking in every detail of her appearance, from the damp coil of hair looped over one shoulder to the shivering aspect of her shapely form. What was he thinking? she wondered. Why was he here? Not to deliver more bad news, she hoped.

It angered her a little that she was even asking herself these questions. Despite his apparent ownership of the site, Luke shouldn't invade her privacy until he had the right to do so. Just because Harley was making a fuss of him, wagging his tail idiotically before rushing up the stairs and evidently expecting them to follow him, didn't mean she had to give in. She sighed when Harley disappeared into the living room. He'd probably gone to fetch his favourite toy for Luke's approval.

'Why are you so wet?' she asked at last, making no move to invite him up to the apartment. But she'd needed to say something, she thought, to ease the tension that was fairly crackling in the air between them.

'I walked from the town square,' he replied harshly. Then, after a nerve-tingling pause, 'Believe it or not, but it's impossible to stay dry when it's raining.'

Sarcastic beast!

Abby wanted to reach past him, open the door and order him to leave. But, of course, she couldn't do that. Not until she'd discovered why he was here.

'I suppose you'd better come up,' she said, indicating the stairs behind her. 'It's cold down here.'

'You think?'

More sarcasm, but Abby chose to ignore it, going ahead of him up the staircase. Nevertheless, she was supremely conscious of him behind her. She was also conscious that she was barefoot, and that the bathrobe only fell a couple of inches below her knees. Not to mention the fact that she was naked underneath.

Her living room had never looked less appealing. The floral fabric of her sofa had seen better days and, although she'd brightened it up with coloured cushions, she was sure Luke would find it very different from what he was used to. Did he still have an apartment? No. He probably owned half a dozen houses by now.

At least Harley, and the lamps she'd switched on around the room, gave the place a homely familiarity. Luke followed her into the room and then closed the door behind him, immediately alerting her to the fact that they were alone.

'Um—perhaps you should take off your jacket,' she said belatedly, and Luke didn't need a second invitation.

'Thanks,' he said, in a voice that implied he'd thought she'd never ask. He draped it over the back of one of the dining chairs. 'It's cold for this time of year.'

'Isn't it?' Abby was glad of the change of tone.

Luke glanced about him. 'Have you lived here long?'

Abby shrugged. 'Over four years,' she replied with some reluctance. 'Why do you want to know?'

Luke's deep-set dark eyes appraised her. 'I'm curious. Is that when you left London?'

Abby shook her head. 'You ask a lot of questions,' she said. 'Why are you here?'

Luke frowned, not answering her, and Abby wondered if she'd ever be able to enter the apartment again without seeing his lean, sardonic figure standing on her hearth.

In a maroon silk shirt, a paler tie pulled a few inches away from his collar, he looked darkly handsome. Add to that charcoal-grey pants, the dampness of which had caused the fabric to cling to his powerful legs, and she doubted any woman could remain immune to his sexual appeal.

She caught her breath, and as she did so Luke spoke again.

'So you stayed with Laurence for over a year after that night in the wine bar,' he remarked provokingly. 'It must have been quite a blow when he threw you out.'

Abby was incensed. 'So that's why you came,' she said disgustedly. 'What are you looking for, Luke? Justification for the way you behaved?'

'The way I behaved?' He sounded incredulous.

'Yes. You couldn't leave it alone, could you? Well, I'm sorry to disappoint you, but I left Harry, not the other way about.'

Luke scowled. 'That's not why I'm here.'

'Well, I can't think of anything else.' She wrapped her robe more closely about her. 'But you've had—what?—four weeks to think of a reason. I'm surprised it took you so long.'

Luke's patience snapped. Without another word, he reached for her, hauling her against him. He didn't care that raindrops were still cascading down his face from his wet hair.

Capturing her chin with one hand, he brought her mouth to his.

Desire, hot and overwhelming, swept over him. His hands sought her hips, pulling her so close she must have been able to feel every muscle and sinew in his aroused body.

Because he was aroused, he realised, feeling his erection throbbing against her stomach. Dear God, what did this woman do to him that when he was with her, he couldn't keep his hands off her?

Abby uttered a small protest, but then she arched against him. Luke was half afraid he was going to climax there and then. Steeling himself against the emotions roiling through his system, he tried to think coherently. He was here to talk about the petition Greg Hughes had no doubt set in motion. Not to make a fool of himself all over again.

But she was so warm, so desirable. Unable to prevent himself, he slid his hands up from her hips to her breasts. With his mouth still devouring hers, he peeled the towelling robe aside.

The belt, already loosely tied, gave way, exposing her naked body to his hungry gaze. Dragging his mouth from hers, he gazed down at her with hungry eyes. 'Oh, yes,' he muttered thickly. 'You're every bit as beautiful as I imagined.'

CHAPTER SIX

ABBY KNEW SHE should pull back. Yet the minute his mouth had captured hers, she'd given in.

She'd known how dangerously attracted to him she was five years ago, and she should have known better. He wasn't even the same man she'd known then. He had become hard and bitter, and he probably despised himself for being here.

He was also immensely successful. And if she wasn't careful, he'd assume that was why she hadn't sent him away.

She looked up into eyes that were dark with desire and something else. Was it resentment? A reluctance to admit what was going on?

She swallowed convulsively. Did she want him to think she was willing to forget the past? Perhaps he imagined she might give herself to him to save the café? Dear God, what was she thinking? This man was her enemy, not her friend.

Yet when his hands caressed her breasts, his thumbs stroking her nipples, making them peak so sharply it was almost painful, her breath quickened wildly.

'You're so beautiful,' he said hoarsely, as if the words were torn from him. 'God help me, I couldn't stay away.'

'Luke—'

'Yes, say my name,' he muttered huskily, lifting the folds of the robe from her shoulders. 'You know I want you, don't you? You've known that right from the start.'

'Well, I don't want you,' she averred unconvincingly, even as her robe fell to the floor.

'I don't believe that,' he responded, sweeping her up into his arms, the yielding flesh beneath his hands belying her protests.

He heard Harley complain as the folds of the robe enveloped him, but by the time the retriever had released himself Luke had crossed the floor to Abby's bedroom.

The lamps were lit, the bed was turned down, and there was a delicious and faintly exotic smell from the adjoining bathroom. Shutting the door with his heel, just in case Harley tried to join them, Luke crossed to the bed and lowered her onto it.

Kicking off his boots, he flung himself beside her. Covering her mouth with his, he thought he would stifle any further protest she might make. But all Abby did was wind her arms about his neck, pulling him even closer, moaning very softly when his tongue invaded her mouth.

Her mouth was just as lush as he remembered. Minutes passed as he continued to kiss her, long, drugging kisses that stirred his body and burned like a fire in his blood.

His fingers sought the hollow behind her ear where her pulse was palpitating wildly; he licked the damp cleavage between her breasts, felt his control slipping as she trembled beneath his hands.

Then she was tearing his shirt free of his trousers, soft fingers probing his waistband, opening his zip. It was a second's job for him to shed his trousers, his breath catching painfully as she caressed the moist tip of his sex.

The realisation that he hadn't brought a condom registered only fleetingly. There was no way he could draw back and go rummaging through his wallet now. As he lay between Abby's parted legs, with Abby urging him to bury himself inside her, sanity finally deserted him. For the first time in his life, he was at the mercy of his desire.

His fingers found her wet core and slipped inside, his thumb massaging the taut nub of her womanhood. She jerked against his hand, moaning uncontrollably, and he could wait no longer.

Without further hesitation, he thrust into her, her muscles expanding and then tightening around him. She arched against him, climaxing almost immediately, and he groaned in protest, the sound vibrating all throughout his chest.

He'd wanted to prolong it, just a few moments longer, to enjoy the sensation of being buried deep inside her. She was so hot, so tight, and his head swam with the intimacy of what was happening.

But the rippling power of her orgasm was too much for him. That, and the sensuous brush of her breasts against his chest, sent him shuddering—helplessly—over the brink.

Someone was licking her face.

Without opening her eyes, Abby put out a protesting hand and touched—hair.

Abby recoiled in surprise, her eyes flying open. Harley was on the bed beside her. It was Harley who had been licking her face, trying to wake her up no doubt. Judging by the urgency with which he jumped off the bed and headed for the open door, he wanted to be let out.

But where was Luke?

Sitting up, she glanced towards the windows. It wasn't quite daylight, but a sliver of silver showed through a crack in the curtains, proving that a grey dawn wasn't far off.

Leaning over, Abby switched on the lamp beside the bed.

She saw by the clock sitting on the bedside cabinet that it wasn't yet five o'clock. Too early to get up in the normal way, but evidently Harley had been disturbed and his needs had to be met.

Sliding her legs out of bed, she shivered as the cool morning air hit her naked body. She guessed her bathrobe was still in the other room; and snatching up a pair of old sweats and a tee shirt, she didn't bother with any underwear before pulling them on.

Where was Luke? she pondered uneasily. The dent in the pillow beside her own surely proved he had slept there. She hadn't been dreaming. Yet Harley had been on the bed when she awoke. He could have trampled the pillow.

But someone had to have opened the bedroom door to let the retriever into the room.

Luke!

The apartment was empty. After slipping on a pair of canvas shoes, Abby followed Harley into the living room. There were no lights burning and there had been when she went to bed—when *they* went to bed, she amended crossly—so Luke had evidently switched them off.

But where was he now?

Harley was still fussing, so, after checking that the rain had stopped, Abby went down a second set of stairs that led into the café. There was a door that gave access to a small garden at the back, and, after letting the retriever out, she stood shivering in the draught.

It would have been easy to think she had imagined the whole thing were it not for the way her body felt. She touched her breasts. They were tender and ultra-sensitive. And between her legs, she ached from the urgency of Luke's possession. She hadn't imagined that shattering climax, or the one that had come after. Nothing so devastating had ever happened to her before.

Certainly not with Harry.

She sucked in a breath. What was she supposed to think? That Luke had come here, taken his pleasure, and departed again without even saying goodbye?

Could he be that insensitive?

Yes.

She'd left the door ajar and it banged open suddenly. She turned, half expecting to see Luke, but it was only Harley bounding inside, looking for his usual treat of a biscuit.

'All right, all right,' she said as he nudged against her leg. 'I wish you could speak, Harls.

You'd be able to tell me what time that jerk walked out.'

The retriever barked once, as if in agreement, and then followed Abby upstairs to the apartment again. In the kitchen, Abby opened the jar containing the dog's biscuits and tossed one to him.

'There you go,' she said as he caught it between his teeth. A sob rose in her throat, but she determinedly swallowed it back. 'At least, I can rely on you.'

Expelling a heavy breath, she filled the coffee filter, and while the water was feeding through the grounds she decided to take a shower. There was no point going back to bed. She knew she wouldn't sleep. Besides, it was light outside. It was already getting on for six o'clock.

In the bathroom, she tried to ignore her reflection without much success. When she'd stripped off her clothes, she groaned at the sight of the stubble burns on her throat and abdomen. There was even faint bruising on her thighs and her tangled hair gave her a wild and abandoned appearance.

Great, she thought. Now all it needed was for one of her customers to notice. Or Greg Hughes, she conceded tensely. He was already suspicious about her relationship with Luke.

In fact, it was her next-door neighbour, Joan Miller, who inadvertently broached the subject.

Abby thought she'd done a good job in hiding the burns Luke had inflicted with his stubble, wearing more make-up than usual and a roll-necked jumper that hid her throat.

And to begin with, her customers were too intent on their own affairs to do much more than wish her a good morning. The rain had started again and most of their comments concerned the unusual coolness of the weather.

Then, after Lori had turned up and they were discussing a new delivery of books that was due to arrive that morning, Joan Miller came into the café and headed towards them.

Joan was a likeable soul, an elderly spinster in her late sixties, who was a good customer of both the café and the bookshop. She read avidly, and knitted copious garments for her sister's grandchildren. And she never seemed to worry that there was no man in her life.

'Oh, Abby,' she said. 'Are you all right? I heard Harley barking last night and I was really tempted to come and see if anything was wrong. But it was raining, and I was sure that if you had a problem, you'd contact me.'

Abby gave an inward groan. Lori was looking speculatively at her now and she knew she had to come up with a convincing excuse.

'Oh, it was just a big spider,' she said, managing a slight laugh. 'You know how Harley hates spiders. He's such a baby.'

'That's all right, then.' Joan smiled in return. 'I did worry that it might be that man Greg was telling me about.'

Abby stared at her. 'What man?'

'Oh, you know. The Morelli man, who came to see you a few weeks ago. Since Greg's started that petition, I've been expecting him to call.'

Abby's lips parted. 'What petition are you talking about?'

'Well, how many petitions are there?' Joan sounded amused now. 'The one to the council, of course, requesting that these properties be granted preservation status. You must have seen it. The last I heard, Greg had over a hundred signatures.'

CHAPTER SEVEN

'So what do you think their chances are?'

Luke was pacing restlessly about Ben Stacey's office in Mayfair, and he paused a moment to fix the other man with an impatient stare.

'Hell, I don't know.' Ben, a man in his early forties, who had worked with Luke for the past four years, gave an indifferent shrug. 'I'm an estate agent, a valuer, Luke. Okay, we occasionally deal with listed buildings, but they're generally of historical or architectural interest. I wouldn't have thought a row of shops that are due for demolition comes into that category.'

'Nor would I,' said Luke with asperity. 'I'm fairly sure this is just a move on Hughes' part to try and get me to pay him increased compensation for having to find new premises for his so-called studio.'

Ben grinned. 'I thought this petition had over a hundred signatures.'

'It does.'

'Well, then.'

'Hughes inaugurated it. I'm sure of it.'

Yet was he? Abby had no reason to think kindly of him either after the way he'd behaved that afternoon when he'd visited the café. And subsequent events...

But he didn't want to think about subsequent events. He especially didn't want to remember how shabbily he'd treated her a week ago. Seducing her, and then walking out on her, had been unforgivable. He'd used her and then made his escape while she was still asleep.

Not that he'd wanted to. It had been one of the hardest things he'd ever done, sliding out of Abby's warm bed. He'd wanted to stay, but that would have been crazy. Did he want her to think he couldn't leave her alone?

But she'd never forgive him, he thought. Hell, he'd never forgive himself. That was not why he'd driven over to Ashford-St-James. He'd wanted to speak to her, yes. To confront her about the petition Felix had told him about. But that was all.

Then, she'd opened the door and he'd seen her, all flushed and warm from her shower, and he'd lost his mind. The lapels of her bathrobe had parted as she'd bent to drag the retriever back into the hall, and he'd glimpsed damp, shadowy cleavage and smelt the fragrant scent of her skin.

God, he could smell it still. It had filled his lungs and interfered with his thought processes, so that by the time he'd got upstairs and into her apartment, he'd been running on nuclear.

'So what are you going to do about it?'

Ben was talking to him now, and Luke, who had been staring blindly out of the fourth-floor windows of his colleague's office, turned a somewhat blank look in his direction.

'Say what?' he asked, his brows drawing together, and Ben gave him a curious look.

'About the petition,' he said patiently. Then he glanced towards the windows himself. 'For pity's sake, what's going on out there? You haven't heard a word I've said for the last five minutes.'

'Oh, sorry.' Luke pulled himself together and offered an apologetic smile. 'I was just wool-gathering, that's all.'

'It must have been some pretty serious wool-gathering, then,' Ben remarked, an amused expression on his face. 'If I had to hazard a guess, I'd say a female was involved.' He paused. 'Am I right?'

Luke pushed a frustrated hand through his dark hair. 'There are women involved in this petition; of course, there are. But so what?' He avoided the other man's eyes. 'In any case, I'd better get going if I want to get anything done today.'

'Okay.' Ben got up from his desk. 'You'll let me know as soon as there are any developments, if you'll excuse the pun?'

'Yeah, right.' Luke shook the other man's hand and headed for the door. 'And if you do happen to run into anyone who knows about these things, perhaps you'd ask him to give me a call.'

'Will do.' Ben grinned, and then added provocatively, 'And give the lady my best, won't you?'

Abby was returning from her usual evening walk with Harley when she saw the sleek silver Bentley parked at the end of the road.

The sky was overcast and once again it was starting to rain, but Abby halted at the sight of the car. No one she wanted to know drove a Bentley. But that didn't alter the fact that it was there.

It was over a week since that evening Luke had come to her apartment. And since then, she'd made it her business to find out all about the petition Greg Hughes had initiated. She guessed that was why Luke had come to see her that evening. Had he wondered if she might be behind it? Surely not.

And yet…

Harley was getting impatient. She'd been standing like a statue for the past couple of minutes and the retriever was waiting for his supper. Was that Luke's car, or was she being paranoid? And even if it was his vehicle, there was more than one property on this block.

The Bentley's door opened and Abby stiffened instinctively. The miserable weather meant there were few people about. She was on her own.

When a man's voice hailed her, her mouth dried. She didn't need to hear Harley's joyful bark of recognition to identify the man. She watched, with a certain amount of trepidation, as Luke swung one leg and then the other out of the car.

It was an effort to hang on to Harley's leash when he wanted so badly to get away, but somehow she managed it. She watched tensely as Luke straightened, pausing for a moment to speak to someone still inside the car. His girlfriend? she wondered, anger stirring. Were all men as unscrupulous as Harry if they could get away with it?

Luke stood there, lean and dark and painfully familiar in a navy business suit, a bronze silk shirt and navy tie. Abby could feel her pulse quickening automatically and despised herself for it. The last time she'd seen him, he'd been naked; his hips pumping urgently between her thighs; his body joined to hers in mutual need.

Or mutual lust, she amended bitterly, steeling herself against the sensual attraction that still had the power to weaken her knees. But he had an incredible nerve coming back here. Did he expect her to behave as if that night over a week ago had never happened?

Now he said coolly, 'Come on, Abby. I'll give you a lift back to the café. You're getting soaked and so am I.'

'An occupational hazard where you're concerned,' she responded tartly. 'What do you want, Luke? If you're worried about the petition, go and speak to Greg.'

Luke stepped away from the car, apparently uncaring that once again his clothes were getting wet, and the retriever went wild with excitement.

Luke saw the problem she was having in controlling him and said impatiently, 'Let him go, Abby. Or do you want to end up with your butt in a puddle?'

Abby ignored him, but she had to pass the car to reach her home. She determinedly avoided looking into the car as she tugged Harley past Luke, but the retriever became so unmanageable, she had to let him go.

In the inevitable melee that ensued, Abby was able to hurry along the street to her door. Fishing her keys out of her pocket, she couldn't prevent a smirk of satisfaction at the thought of what the retriever's paws might do to that expensive suit.

She had to leave the door open for Harley. She had no doubt the dog would find his way home, if only because his supper was due. Kicking off her wet shoes, she picked them up and hurried up the stairs to the apartment. She didn't think even Luke would have the nerve to follow her there.

Going into the kitchen, she took off her coat and draped it over a chair. It would dry in the warmth, once she put the pizza she'd bought for her own supper in the oven. A rub-down with a towel was all Harley would need.

She avoided looking at her reflection in the mirror above the fireplace. But her bedraggled braid and pale face drew her eyes. So what? she thought, smoothing her hair with rain-wet fingers. Why should she care what she looked like? It wasn't as if she wanted Luke to show any interest in her again.

She heard the downstairs door bang back on its hinges.

Harley, she conceded, hearing the retriever pounding up the stairs. His paws pattered over the carpet, no doubt heading for his water bowl. He was always thirsty after a walk.

She would have to go and close the door, and she hoped Luke had got the message. If he was hanging about outside, waiting for an invitation to come in, hard luck.

But when she got to the top of the stairs and looked down, she saw Luke standing in the hallway. He was dripping water onto her doormat, his shoulder braced carelessly against the frame.

Luke saw the indignant expression that crossed Abby's face when she saw him. But, hell, surely she hadn't expected him to wait outside?

Yet that was probably where he belonged, he mused grimly. He was still despising himself for coming here, but he'd had to see her again. If only to prove that he'd exaggerated the effect she'd had on him; exaggerated the chemistry between them that was interfering with his sleep.

But, looking up at her, he had the distinct feeling he hadn't.

She was wearing jeans tonight, tight jeans that clung to her long legs and accentuated the provocative curve of her bottom. Her shirt was olive green and unfastened at the neck, exposing the delicious hollow between her breasts. She was wearing little make-up, but she didn't need any. Her skin was as smooth and soft as a peach.

Without giving her a chance to tell him to get out, he said quietly, 'May I come up? I'd like to talk to you.'

'Why ask me?' said Abby coldly. 'You seem to do exactly as you like whatever I say.'

'Abby…' He sighed, and then turned to close and lock the door before climbing the stairs. 'I know I've upset you—'

'You think?'

'—but there are things we need to say to one another.'

'Really?' Abby turned as he reached her and went back into the apartment. 'Goodbye would be a good beginning.'

Luke shook his head, and, ignoring her words, he closed the living-room door behind him. Then, turning back to watch her as she went into the kitchen, he said, 'I know I behaved like a heel the last time I was here. At least let me say, I'm sorry.'

Abby took a bag of what appeared to be dog food out of the cupboard. Then she bent to fill the retriever's food bowl.

'There you go, Harls,' she said, her tone much different from when she'd spoken to Luke. 'You're hungry, aren't you?'

Luke moved across the room. 'Are you hungry, too?'

'What's it to you? I'm not inviting you for supper.'

'I know that.' Luke blew out a frustrated breath. 'I was going to invite you to have dinner with me.'

Abby's eyes met his. 'You're not serious?'

'I am.' Luke hesitated. 'According to my father, there's a pub in the next village that serves a decent steak. At least let me do something to show you I'm not the selfish bastard you evidently think I am.'

'You think buying me a steak will do that?' Abby was incredulous.

'No. But it might go some way to showing you I regret the way I behaved.'

Abby's lips twisted. 'And, of course, this has nothing to do with the petition, which you've obviously heard about? Are you sure you're not just here on a fact-finding mission again?'

Luke scowled. 'Dammit, my invitation has nothing to do with Hughes' petition.'

'No?'

'No.' He stared into her disbelieving eyes, aware that what he really wanted to do was to touch her. 'I'd like the chance to talk to you without Harley, or one of your customers, interrupting us.'

CHAPTER EIGHT

ABBY HESITATED.

She knew she ought to refuse—that she *should* refuse—but she defended her right to change her mind.

Taking a breath, she said, 'What do you want to talk about?' Her lips twisted. 'We could have talked the other morning, but you couldn't wait to get out of here.'

'Would you have wanted your neighbours to see me leaving before you opened the café, and come to the obvious conclusion?' he demanded tersely.

Abby gave a disbelieving laugh. 'You're not telling me you left here in the middle of the night to protect my reputation?'

He had the decency to colour. 'Not exactly.'

'Not at all,' she corrected him scornfully. 'I'm amazed you had the nerve to come back.'

'Which should tell you something about my character,' he retorted. 'Come on, Abby. Give me a break.'

'I'm not ready,' she said, buying time to think about the craziness of accepting his invitation. 'And you've got wet marks on your trousers.'

'I'll dry,' said Luke easily. 'And you look pretty good to me.'

Abby gave him a conservative look. 'Yeah, right.'

'I mean it.' His eyes darkened. 'You can't have any doubts that I'm sincere after we slept together.'

Abby hesitated. 'I'm not going to sleep with you again.'

'Okay.' She suspected Luke would have agreed to anything in this mood. 'Will you come for dinner with me?'

'I need a shower,' she said, half hoping he would lose patience and leave.

'Have it later,' Luke advised flatly, tucking his cold hands under his arms. 'It's raining, as you know.' He paused. 'Humour me, Abby. You're going to get wet, anyway.'

Abby could have argued some more, but her heart wasn't really in it. Where was the harm? she asked herself. She was a grown woman, not a child. Didn't he owe her something for the way he'd behaved?

Or was she only making excuses to spend more time with a man she knew she should despise?

'Okay,' she said at last, heading towards her bedroom. 'I won't be a minute. I just want to tidy my hair.'

But she closed the door securely, letting him hear the latch click into place, before going into the bathroom. No matter how she tried to justify what she was doing, she couldn't deny the fear that if he followed her, they'd end up in bed again.

Fool!

Downstairs, with Harley not-so-happily secured in the living room of the apartment, Abby suddenly remembered that Luke hadn't been alone. She knew she hadn't mistaken the way he'd spoken to someone in the car as he was getting out.

'Wait,' she said, touching his sleeve as he was opening the outer door. 'You've not come on your own, have you? And if it's one of your girlfriends—'

'I don't have girlfriends,' muttered Luke irritably, shaking off her hand. 'Come and meet Felix.' He opened the door and to her surprise Abby found the Bentley waiting outside, apparently indifferent to the 'No Parking' signs.

As they approached the driver's side door opened and a man got out. He was older than Luke, but not by a lot; thin and balding, with a likeable face, he was dressed all in black.

He grinned when he saw them and came round to open the rear door. 'Good evening, miss,' he said politely, evidently waiting for her to get inside. 'Crappy evening, isn't it?'

Abby's lips parted in surprise, and Luke grinned, too. 'Don't mind Felix,' he said humorously. 'He forgets he's in service.'

Abby shook her head. 'He works for you?'

'Sure does,' said Luke, following her into the back of the vehicle. 'Meet Felix Laidlaw, chauffeur, butler, and even cook on occasion. Isn't that right, Felix?'

'If you say so.' Felix's tone was non-committal. 'But don't take what he says too seriously, miss. Luke and I go way back. And we were in the services in those days. The real services, isn't that right, Luke?'

If Abby hadn't been looking at him at that moment, she'd have missed Luke's grimace. But with the door still open, the interior light was on in the car. And she noticed the way Luke's brows drew together, as if warning Felix not to go on.

But he did.

'Saved my life, he did. In Afghanistan. Must be over ten years ago now, right, Luke?'

Luke's frown had turned into a scowl. 'Just drive,' he said, slamming the car door and successfully hiding his expression. 'The Bell, in Chitterford. I think you know it.'

Evidently Felix wasn't offended and he kept up a stream of small talk until they reached their destination.

Actually, Abby was grateful. It removed any need for her to make conversation, and judging by the way Luke stared out of the car's windows for the whole of the journey, he felt the same.

The Bell turned out to be a small pub, whose restaurant had a big reputation. As soon as they stepped through the door they were assailed by the most delicious smell of food. And although Abby had been sure she had no appetite, the dishes on offer were too tantalising to refuse.

The chauffeur wasn't with them, of course. Luke had said he would give the man a ring when they were ready to leave, and Felix had appeared happy with that arrangement.

They were shown to a table for two. The crisp white tablecloth and the bud vase of roses were complemented by a lamp with a rose-coloured shade.

'This is lovely,' said Abby, glancing about her. Anything to avoid looking into Luke's eyes. 'Have you been here before?'

'No, but my father has,' replied Luke as a waitress came to ask if they would like a drink before their meal. Then, apparently remembering her liking for white wine, he ordered a glass of chardonnay for her and a beer for himself.

The waitress departed and Abby nodded. 'Of course. You said your father lives in Bath,' she continued, hoping to keep the conversation light. 'It seems very nice.'

'So do you,' said Luke in a dangerously bland tone, bringing an immediate flush of heat to her cheeks.

'You don't have to say that,' she said shortly, annoyed with herself for allowing anything he said to disconcert her. Then, determinedly, 'Tell me about Felix.'

'What do you want to know?'

Abby gave him an enquiring look. 'Oh, I don't know,' she said casually. 'How you saved his life, perhaps?'

'Felix exaggerates.'

'Does he?' Abby arched an inquiring brow. 'I didn't get that impression.'

'The helicopter I was flying had to ditch in southern Afghanistan,' he said shortly. 'Felix was hurt, and I dragged him out of the aircraft.'

'Was it on fire?'

Luke's mouth turned down. 'Don't make me out to be a hero, Abby.'

Abby stared at him. 'But you can fly a helicopter?'

Luke shook his head. 'Let's talk about something else.' He paused. 'Do your parents live near Ashford?'

'No.' Abby hesitated. Then she said, 'My father was killed in a car accident when I was five, and my mother died—a few years ago.'

'I'm sorry.' Luke sounded as if he meant it. There was a moment's silence, then he picked up the menu the waitress had left. 'So—what would you like to eat?'

It was difficult to choose, but Abby finally settled on avocado and prosciutto, followed by sea bass, with a scallop and butter sauce. When the waitress returned with their drinks, Luke gave the order, barely glancing at the menu before ordering the avocado, too, and a steak.

Once again, there was silence for a few minutes, and then Abby, who had been tasting her wine, said, 'How about you? You said your father lives in Bath, but you didn't mention your mother.'

'That's because my mother doesn't live with us,' replied Luke tersely. 'She walked out when I was ten years old. My father's not a poor man, but my mother found herself a man with more money than he had.'

'So do you see her now?'

'No.' Luke clearly didn't want to talk about it. 'The last I heard, she was on her fourth husband. I don't know where the hell she is and I don't particularly care.'

Abby suspected he did care as she absorbed his words.

She hesitated and then ventured daringly, 'Is that why you've never married?'

The vehemence of his response startled her. 'I've been married, Abby,' he said bitterly. 'As a matter of fact, I married the girl I'd been going out with before you came on the scene.'

'Ah.' Now it was Abby's turn to be confused. She pressed her lips together before saying challengingly, 'So you weren't free when we met either.'

Luke's expression darkened. 'Oh, I was free, Abby. I didn't do commitment. Anyone could have told you that.'

'Then—'

'But I was stupid enough to think that you were as innocent as you looked.' He snorted. 'And then, guess what? I found out you weren't.'

Abby didn't say anything and after a few moments he went on, 'The marriage didn't last. Like I said, I don't do commitment. But Sonia didn't suffer by it. I'm pretty sure she'd checked out my bank balance before she accepted my ring.'

Abby shook her head. 'You're very cynical.'

'Do you blame me? I guess you're going to tell me that you're not.'

'I hope I'm not,' said Abby at once. 'And I probably have more reason to be so than you.'

Luke regarded her scornfully. 'I'm sure you believe you can justify what you did. Forgive me, if I don't shed any tears on your behalf.'

Abby pressed her lips together. She was tempted to walk out of the restaurant at that moment, but the waitress returned with their food and she felt obliged to stay in her seat.

Instead, she had to content herself with glaring at him until the woman had gone. Then she said grimly, 'Do you really think I'll stay and eat with you after that?'

Luke sighed. 'I'm not going to apologise for what I said.'

'I wouldn't expect you to.' She paused. 'I'll get a taxi to take me home.'

But when she would have got up from her seat, Luke put out a hand and restrained her.

'Okay,' he said. 'I shouldn't have brought up all that old stuff now. But you started it, asking about my mother. *She* almost ruined my father's life.'

Abby's tongue appeared to moisten her lips. 'And that's your excuse?'

'Yeah.'

'Are you implying that I almost ruined your life?'

He looked taken aback at that. 'Uh, no,' he

muttered unwillingly. Then his hand tightened on her wrist and Abby felt the undeniable rush of awareness. 'Don't go,' he said huskily, and heat like liquid fire ran through her blood. 'Whatever happened in the past, I still want you.'

Abby looked down at the lean brown hand gripping her wrist and felt her stomach tighten. It was useless to pretend she didn't want him, too.

But want and *need* were two very different bedfellows. An appalling pun, she acknowledged, but this time she intended to keep her head.

Withdrawing her wrist with an effort, she said quietly, 'What do you expect me to do, Luke?'

'Stay,' he said at once. 'If I promise to behave, we could try and enjoy the evening. The food smells good, you must admit, and, despite words to the contrary, I do enjoy your company.'

'Do you?'

His eyes consumed her. 'You know I do.'

Abby expelled an uneven breath. 'All right,' she said, almost convinced she was going to regret this. 'It would be a shame to waste the food.'

'Your magnanimity is overwhelming,' he said drily, and then raised a hand, palm towards her, when she looked as if she was about to protest again. 'Eat. And drink your wine. What is it they say? Alcohol has charms to soothe the savage beast?'

'I think that was music,' said Abby, unable to deny a small smile. 'But I must admit, this wine is really delicious.'

After such a contentious beginning, surprisingly the hours they stayed at the pub were some of the most enjoyable Abby had ever spent.

When he wasn't being provocative or sarcastic, Luke was really good company. But she'd known that, she mused, remembering the first night she'd met him at the wine bar.

She could have loved him, she thought rather wistfully; would have divorced her abusive husband in a heartbeat, if her mother's circumstances hadn't been so grave.

Felix drove them back to Ashford-St-James soon after ten o'clock. Abby had confessed she had to be up by five a.m. the next morning, to get to the wholesalers to pick up supplies. And when she added that she had to prepare the scones and muffins, and set the coffee machine in operation before she opened the café at seven-thirty, Luke understood her desire not to be out too late.

However, when they got back to her apartment, she felt obliged to invite him in for coffee. They hadn't waited to have coffee at the restaurant, and she knew it was the least she could do after such a delicious meal.

'Felix, too, if you like,' she added, half hoping the chauffeur would join them.

But Felix demurred, saying he was going for a late supper at a fast-food establishment. And Luke said he would ring him again when he was ready to leave.

Abby was glad of Harley to provide a distraction when they got into the apartment. The retriever was eager to greet their visitor, and he threaded his way around Luke's legs, uttering little woofs of pleasure.

Meanwhile, Abby went into the kitchen and set the water running through the filter. It would have been easier to make instant, but it didn't smell half so nice.

Only belatedly did she become aware that Luke had come into the kitchen, too, and was now standing, hips propped against one of the units. He'd loosened his tie and unfastened the top button on his shirt; his forearms, lightly spread with dark hair, bare below rolled-back cuffs.

When had he removed his jacket? she wondered. Did he feel he had the right to be here? And why, when he was fully dressed in his navy suit trousers and that very attractive bronze silk shirt, was she picturing him without any clothes at all?

Because he was so damn sexy, she thought, dragging her eyes away and concentrating on the coffee. She'd managed to ignore—or at least, *control*—her instinctive attraction to him all evening. Was it too much to ask that she do it just a little while longer?

However, here, alone in her apartment—apart from Harley, of course—her whole body felt hot and sensually alive.

And overwhelmingly aware of her own physical needs, however unwelcome those needs might be.

And because of that, her voice was a little sharp when she said, 'Why don't you go and sit down?' She paused and then added shortly, 'You're making me nervous.'

Luke arched a dark brow. 'Am I?'

'You know you are,' she said tightly. 'Do you get some pleasure out of annoying people?'

Luke stared at her now. 'Did I miss something here? What did I do to deserve that?'

Abby's lips tightened. 'Nothing,' she said, realising how unreasonable she was being. 'You did nothing. I suppose I'm tired, that's all. It's been a long day.'

'And you want me to leave, is that it?'

Leave? *No!*

She looked up from setting out the cups, and met his dark gaze. And knew she was treading on dangerous ground.

'You—you must do what you think best,' she said, not sure where this was leading. 'Stay or go, it's all the same to me.'

CHAPTER NINE

IT WASN'T, OF COURSE, and when Luke spoke again, she realised her mistake.

'What if I said I wanted to go to bed with you?' he asked casually, straightening away from the unit. 'Would I get what I want then?'

Abby caught her breath. 'I told you at the start of the evening—'

'Yeah, I know what you told me at the start of the evening,' he muttered. 'Okay.' He stepped aside as she picked up a tray containing the two cups of coffee she'd prepared. 'Let's have coffee like civilised human beings.'

Abby carried the tray into the living room and set it on the low table in front of the hearth. It meant she was obliged to sit on the sofa, with its multi-coloured cushions. Cushions that were liberally coated with dog hair, she noticed, but Luke didn't seem to mind.

Predictably, he seated himself beside her, the cushions tipping sideways beneath his weight.

Abby shifted to the edge of the seat to keep her balance, before leaning forward to hand Luke his cup.

'Thanks.'

Luke took the coffee and then said, somewhat sarcastically, 'Isn't this cosy? To think I almost turned you down.'

'Did you?' He was almost sure she didn't believe him. 'So I suppose you can understand why I'll be so sorry to leave this place?'

Luke blew out a breath. 'I see. So you really invited me in to talk about the petition, did you?' He set his cup on the tray again. 'I assume yours is one of the over one hundred signatures Hughes is supposed to have?'

Abby stared at him. 'Actually, no,' she said shortly. 'I didn't know anything about the petition until Joan Miller told me what was going on.'

Luke's brows drew together. 'Am I supposed to believe that?'

'You can believe what you like,' she retorted hotly. 'I'm not a liar.'

'But you agree with its sentiments, surely,' Luke persisted, spreading his legs and resting his forearms along his thighs. He glanced sideways at her. 'You've just said how sorry you'll be to leave.'

Abby sighed. 'I will be sorry to leave,' she admitted. 'But I don't know anything about Greg's petition. He evidently didn't think I would be prepared to sign it.'

Luke regarded her curiously. 'And why would he think that?'

She pulled a wry face. 'Why do you think?'

'I don't know. That's why I'm asking you.'

Clearly she didn't believe him, but she said patiently, 'Because he thinks I'm a—a friend of yours, I suppose.' She shook her head. 'He's not a fool. He could tell we'd known one another before you turned up at the café.'

'So what did you tell him?'

Abby put down her own cup, afraid he would notice how her hands were shaking. 'I didn't tell him anything,' she stated flatly. 'What was I supposed to say? That we'd met five years ago in a wine bar? That you were in danger of defending my honour, before discovering I was an unfaithful wife?'

She paused. 'Or would you rather I told him that you took your revenge by seducing me here a week ago? That you—how is it the romantic novelists put it?—that you had your wicked way with me, and then walked out without even saying goodbye?'

Luke straightened. 'That's not true!'

'What's not true? You did have sex with me.'

He scowled. 'By no means could you call it having my wicked way with you, Abby. You didn't exactly push me away.'

Abby got up from the sofa. 'I think you'd better go.'

'Why?' He looked up at her, his dark eyes impaling hers. He waited a beat and then added softly, 'Don't you like the direction our conversation is going? Can you honestly say you didn't want me as much as I wanted you?'

Abby moved towards the door, ordering Harley to stay where he was without a lot of success. 'Just go,' she said, turning away as if she couldn't bear to look at him. 'It's too late to be having this discussion now.'

'Oh, I agree.'

Luke got to his feet and went after her. Ignoring Harley's bid for attention, he caught Abby's arms and jerked her back against him, burying his face in the scented hollow at her nape. 'Abby, let's stop arguing. You have no idea what you do to me.'

Abby knew what he did to her, and she caught her breath. 'Don't do this, Luke!' The word *please* hovered on the tip of her tongue, but she managed to hold it back.

'Why not?' His tongue sought the pulse beating rapidly below her ear and he let one hand stroke sensuously over her cheek. His thumb found her mouth, parted her lips and pushed inside. 'Can you honestly say this isn't what you really want?'

Abby couldn't prevent her tongue from seeking his thumb, couldn't deny the hunger growing deep in her belly. Luke was like an addiction, she thought. Now that she'd tasted his lovemaking, she wanted to taste it again.

And how pitiful was that?

His hand moved to her breast, massaging the erect peak through the fabric of her shirt. Emotions that wouldn't be denied stirred inside her. Where would be the harm in giving in to him? she asked herself crazily. Why was she denying herself the simple pleasure of his touch?

'Do you want me to go?' he asked huskily, his free hand sliding possessively along her jaw, turning her mouth to his.

And, God help her, she didn't try to resist him this time. She let his lips capture hers and let her mouth accept the hungry invasion of his tongue.

Her head swam. But it wasn't the fault of the wine she'd drunk earlier. The feelings his kiss aroused caused a sensual dizziness she couldn't control. His heat, hot and thick, enveloped her, wrapping her in a cocoon of need that it was virtually impossible to deny.

Her hands slid up his chest, feeling the quickening beat of his heart. His silk shirt moved sensuously against her palms, and she clutched a handful greedily. She was drowning in physical sensation, losing any sense of who she was. Who *he* was.

'Abby,' he protested hoarsely, when she tore open two of his shirt buttons and pressed her lips against his chest.

Abby ignored him. She'd discovered that his skin was damp and salty and lightly spread with dark hair. It reminded her unmistakeably of the way it arrowed down below his navel, cradling the swollen pressure of his sex.

God knew, he was a temptation, and she was not immune to the memories that she'd denied for so long.

Memories of him all those years ago, kissing her in his car in the car park at the apartments where she'd lived with Harry. Memories of how nervous she'd been when she'd made that call. Memories of how he'd looked in the wine bar, when Harry had told him what a fool he'd been in trusting her…

And what was she doing now? Did she want him to think she was that easy? Because, truth to tell, she probably was where he was concerned.

His kiss hardened and deepened, and he dragged her closer against him, so she could feel every taut muscle behind his zip. One of his legs pushed between hers, forcing her nearer. And she could feel the wetness inside her panties and the ultra-sensitive pressure of her sex against his thigh.

Harley whined, and she was brought unwillingly to her senses. Evidently the retriever didn't like being neglected, or perhaps he was trying to remind her of what had happened before.

She shouldn't run away with the idea that because Luke wanted her, he didn't still believe she had stayed with Harry because he could keep her in the luxurious manner to which she'd become accustomed. He still thought she'd been a rich bitch, looking for diversion.

If he only knew. If only he'd let her explain…

But she'd tried that once before without any success.

In addition to which, she mustn't forget that he was also prepared to deprive her—and the other leaseholders—of their livelihoods. She shouldn't expect any special favours from a man like him.

Catching her breath, she drew back and managed to put a little space between them. Then, swallowing, she said, 'Can we talk?'

Luke's brows drew together, and he raked back his tumbled hair with a slightly unsteady hand. 'You're not serious.'

'I am.'

'Abby, you do know what's going on here?' His own face was flushed, and there was impatience in his tone. 'What in God's name do you want to talk to me about right now?'

Abby stared at him. 'I want to talk about Harry.'

'You're kidding!' He stared at her disbelievingly. 'I thought we dealt with that earlier.'

'Well, you were wrong.' She caught her lower lip between her teeth. '*I* was wrong. I have to tell you why I stayed with him when—'

'Oh, not that again.' Now Luke linked both hands at the back of his neck and stared at her with bitter eyes. 'I *know* why you stayed with Laurence, Abby.'

'No, you don't.'

'I'm not a fool, Abby. The guy was a cash cow. You're not the first woman to marry a man for his money.'

'You couldn't be more wrong.'

'Couldn't I?' He paused. 'Just don't think I'm in the market for that kind of relationship. I was cured of that five years ago.'

Abby gasped. 'You bastard!'

'I've been called that before. I think it's getting a little old?'

Abby stared at him. 'So—you seriously expect I would be willing to be your mistress?'

'Why not?' He spoke succinctly, and she

clenched her fists so tightly, her nails dug into her palms.

'Just because I let you make love to me the last time you were here does not make me your whore!' she retorted angrily, despising herself and him in equal measure.

'Did I use that word?' Luke regarded her narrowly, his eyes watching her intently.

'You didn't have to.'

'Well, forgive me,' he said sarcastically. 'Only it's hard to feel sympathy for a woman who's cheated on her husband in the past.'

'You know nothing about my marriage to Harry.'

'And I don't want to know,' he retorted, reaching for his jacket. 'Perhaps you're right. Perhaps I should get out of here.'

'Perhaps you should,' said Abby, striving for indifference.

But before Luke could grab his jacket and leave, his strong fingers trailed down her sleeve and flipped beneath the hem of her shirt. She tried to back away from him, but the temptation of Luke's touch was too much for her.

And when his hand spread against her bare midriff, warm and possessive against her soft flesh, every nerve in her body went on high alert. She wanted him to touch her, she admitted despairingly. Her limbs were melting in anticipation of his caress.

Without giving her a chance to break his hold, he pulled her down onto the sofa again and, pressing her back, covered her body with his.

Then, possessing her mouth, he whispered arrogantly, 'What was it you were saying about not wanting to be my mistress?'

CHAPTER TEN

LUKE WAS IN a foul mood when he got back from Edinburgh.

The weather had been predictably bad and the conference he'd attended had been boring in the extreme. In addition to which, he'd spent much of the last three days fending off the advances of his host's daughter, who seemed to think she was God's gift to the opposite sex.

Fortunately, he'd had Felix drive him to the conference, so he hadn't had to suffer the girl's unsubtle attention on the flight back. She apparently worked in London, too, but he'd made sure she was never in a position to suggest he gave her a lift back to the capital.

Nevertheless, Luke found the return journey long and tedious. He'd worked on his laptop for a while, but, when he'd achieved as much as could be achieved without his files, he'd spent the remainder of the journey staring out of the window at the motorway.

Felix had done his best to entertain him, but he'd received monosyllabic replies at best. And, after a while, he'd asked Luke if he'd mind if he put on some music.

Luke had offered no objections, but he had raised the screen between the two halves of the car, which had been answer enough for Felix. The music had been turned off and silence had reigned until they got back to Eaton Close.

Back home, Luke took a shower and changed into casual clothes. His housekeeper, Mrs Webb, had prepared a delicious dinner for him, but, although he ate the smoked salmon, he only picked at the braised belly of pork, and didn't touch the chocolate mousse.

She tutted her disapproval as she cleared the table in the morning room. The room overlooked the terraced garden at the back of the house, which at present was a riot of colour. A teak bench sat in the shade of hydrangeas and semi-tropical ferns that Luke's gardener kept in immaculate order.

Mrs Webb knew better than to make any verbal complaint about his appetite, however, and asked if Luke would like coffee in the library.

'Yeah, sure,' said Luke, pushing away from the table. He forced a polite smile. 'Sounds good.'

Even so, the word 'coffee' aroused disturbing connotations in his mind. It might be several weeks since that night in Ashford-St-James, when he'd gone to Abby's apartment; but the memory was all too vivid, reminding him, as it had done before, that his behaviour where she was concerned was less than commendable.

He asked himself for the umpteenth time why he'd gone to see her again. It wasn't as if he'd had any intention of pursuing their affair. Indeed, his original idea had been to prove he was not the man she evidently thought he was.

And what a waste of time that had been.

He supposed he could make the excuse that he'd wanted to apologise, for the way he'd behaved the last time they were together. But as soon as he'd seen her, as soon as she'd shown her indifference towards him, his pride had kicked in. In consequence, his good intentions had gone out of the window along with his common sense.

Nonetheless, he had enjoyed having dinner with her. Too much, he suspected, which was why he was in the position he was in now. He'd let her get under his skin again and he'd done what any red-blooded man would have done and had sex with her.

Hot, passionate sex, as it happened. The kind of sex, he acknowledged, that he couldn't put out of his mind.

She'd just been so damnably desirable. He hadn't been able to keep his hands off her. But was that any excuse for what had happened?

Probably not.

When they'd parted, he hadn't asked if he could see her again. Despite the fact that he really hadn't wanted to leave. But Felix had been waiting, and he'd told himself he had nothing to be ashamed of. She'd been as eager to be with him as he had been with her.

But he should have at least followed up the encounter with a phone call.

The truth was, he disliked the fact that she still had such an effect on him. That had never happened before with any woman, and it disturbed him.

Goodness knew, the past few weeks had been hectic, and he shouldn't have had time to think of anything else but the business. There'd been strategy board meetings, budget discussions, and financial seminars, all demanding his attention. And that without this most recent interminable conference in Edinburgh that he'd not been able to avoid.

He should have been able to forget about Abby. It wasn't as if she were an angel. Quite the reverse, he assured himself, considering the way she'd treated her husband. Yet she consistently continued to occupy his thoughts.

* * *

Abby woke up with a thumping headache.

She wasn't used to getting headaches or the unpleasant feeling of nausea that gripped her as soon as she got out of bed. This wasn't the first time she'd felt sick and she didn't like it. Oh, Lord, she thought, I hope I'm not getting flu. There was a lot of it about, despite it being the middle of August.

But perhaps the fact that it was the middle of August, and it had been fairly humid recently, might account for her headache. Although she was used to these early mornings, there were times recently when she'd have liked to stay in bed.

Unfortunately, that wasn't possible. So long as she was running the café on her own, and so long as she hadn't received notice to vacate the premises, she had to go on as if nothing was going to change.

The room swam about her as she went into the bathroom, and she only just made it to the toilet before throwing up. This was a first, but fortunately she didn't have a lot in her stomach. She'd only had beans on toast for her supper the night before, but by the time she'd struggled up from her knees she was firmly convinced she'd never eat baked beans again.

Conversely, she felt considerably better after being sick.

She showered and dressed and hurried downstairs to let Harley out into the back garden. He seemed to sense that something was amiss this morning and fussed about her. But he did as he was told, and she gave him a reassuring hug as well as his usual biscuit treat.

Then, after taking him back up to the apartment for his breakfast, she hurried downstairs again to set the coffee machine working. Because she was a little later than usual, she didn't stop to have any breakfast, contenting herself with a cup of tea from the hot-water tap on the coffee machine.

At least she didn't have to go to the wholesalers today. She could get started on the baking right away. But, unfortunately, the smell of the dough caused the nauseous feeling to return, and she was forced to prepare a slice of dry toast to calm her unsettled stomach.

Once again, she felt considerably better after eating the toast, and she was able to complete her usual baking schedule without further delay. She really ought to consider taking on an assistant, other than Lori, she thought as she took a batch of muffins out of the oven. And then realised how ludicrous that thought was.

In a matter of months, there'd be no café to

worry about. Instead of making plans to hire an assistant, she ought to be giving some serious consideration to where she was going to live— and work—after the café was demolished.

But, in all honesty, she'd deliberately avoided thinking about her future since she'd realised Luke didn't intend to see her again. It was some weeks now, and he hadn't even picked up the phone.

She should never have invited him in, she acknowledged with hindsight. She'd known she was asking for trouble. But after the evening they'd spent, it had seemed churlish to turn him away.

Or that had been her excuse at the time, she conceded. Besides, if she was totally honest with herself, she hadn't wanted the evening to end.

What an idiot she was! Telling him she wouldn't be his mistress, and then allowing him to make love to her on the sofa of all places. She couldn't even make the excuse that he'd swept her into his arms and carried her into the bedroom. They'd been so eager to get one another's clothes off, if the sofa hadn't been available, they'd have made love on the floor.

And that was the truth.

Besides, she shouldn't blame him for her weaknesses. Breathless and barely sensible, she'd have done anything he asked of her. She'd wanted him and when he'd imitated with his fingers what he wanted to do to her body, her blood had turned to fire in her veins.

Abby remembered her head had swum long before he'd lowered his head and his tongue had taken the place of his hand. She'd wanted to protest, but her legs had parted willingly. She remembered gripping handfuls of his hair when he'd pressed his face between her legs, and she'd come before she could stop herself.

Afterwards, Luke had slid smoothly into her, and although she'd been sure she wouldn't come again, she had. Just feeling his shaft stretching her and filling her had excited her beyond measure, and when he'd spilled his seed inside her, she'd shared his release.

Goodness knew what Harley must have thought, hearing the sobbing cries she'd been making. But he'd evidently decided Luke wouldn't do her any harm. At some point, he'd slunk away into the bedroom, and she thought rather ruefully what a poor excuse for a guard dog he'd proved to be.

At least this time Luke hadn't walked out on her. Or so she'd convinced herself in the early hours of the morning, after he'd said goodbye.

His parting kiss had convinced her she would see him again. She'd known he was still semi-aroused, and she was fairly sure he hadn't wanted to leave. But poor old Felix had been waiting outside and she'd had to let him go.

At times, it seemed both her past and her future were tied up with that man. He had influenced her life five years ago, and he was influencing it still.

After all, his involvement had had a disastrous effect on her marriage. Although, that really hadn't been his fault. She'd been the one to risk her marriage vows. And, she had paid for that one mistake. Her ex-husband had seen to that.

Now, it seemed, Luke was having a similarly destructive effect on her present. Which didn't seem entirely fair. But she wasn't the only one to suffer this time. And she should be grateful Luke wasn't using her indiscretions against her friends.

When she'd decided to move to Ashford-St-James, it had been with the intention of putting her unhappy marriage behind her. She'd never expected to have to face either Luke or Harry again.

And she was fairly sure Luke hadn't expected to have to face her either. When he'd walked into the café that first morning, he'd been as shocked as she'd been herself.

What were the odds? she mused, shaking her head as she unloaded another batch of muffins onto a cooling tray. Life could be so unpredictable. Not to mention needlessly cruel.

At another time, in another place, she and Luke might have had the chance to become more than occasional lovers. She liked to think so. She couldn't deny that when they were together, she couldn't think of anything but him. He filled her, both mentally and physically. He took over her life—and her body—to the exclusion of anyone else.

Did she love him?

The thought came out of nowhere.

She sighed. The fact was, five years ago, she could have loved him; she knew that. That was why she'd done something she'd never done before. She'd phoned a man who wasn't her husband. Phoned him late in the evening, and asked him to meet her somewhere she'd been sure Harry would never go.

It had taken a lot of courage to actually pick up the phone in the first place. But after the row she'd had with Harry, she'd been desperate to speak to another human being; someone who wouldn't turn every word she'd uttered into a threat.

Harry had become an expert at that. He'd always said he couldn't trust her, but now she could see he'd used that as a way to justify his own behaviour.

That night, after his making more ridiculous accusations about her behaviour, she'd been half afraid he was going to kill her. He'd evidently enjoyed frightening her, but, when he'd put his hands around her throat, she'd suspected even Harry had been alarmed by his own violence. He'd stormed out of the apartment, telling her he was going to his club and not to expect him back before morning, leaving her, as he'd done many times before, shaken and afraid.

For a few minutes after his departure, Abby remembered she'd lain on the floor where he'd left her, too numb to move. She'd heard the door slam, but she couldn't be sure he wasn't still in the apartment. He'd pretended to leave on other occasions and then come back to catch her out.

But, eventually, grateful that she was still alive, she'd forced herself to her feet and dragged herself into the bathroom. She'd wanted to examine her injuries. To reassure herself that there was no blood. It was rare that Harry left any visible signs of his cruelty on her body, but tonight he seemed to have lost all control.

As well as the bruising on her arms and ribs and abdomen, there'd been purple finger marks on her neck. Touching them, flinching from the pain, she'd felt sick inside. She'd ached in every part of her body, and she'd been afraid he wouldn't stop until she was dead.

For a while she'd simply stood in the shower, trying to wipe the memory of the last couple of hours from her mind. She'd run the shower hot, to erase the chill inside her, but not even the stream of water had seemed to work.

Then she'd remembered the card Luke Morelli had given her. She'd stepped out of the shower and stumbled into the bedroom, hoping she still knew where it was.

Stereotypically, she'd hidden it beneath her underwear, and she'd been half afraid Harry might have searched her drawers and found it. But, despite his accusations, her husband had never really believed there was any chance of her being unfaithful to him. He'd known she was too afraid of what it might mean to her mother. He'd never doubted the power he had over her because of Annabel Lacey's illness.

Meeting Luke that night had been the most reckless thing she'd ever done. She'd never forget the thrill it had given her to find him at the Parker House, waiting for her.

Tall and dark and undeniably gorgeous.

She'd just wanted to throw herself into his arms…

Later that morning, Lori came through from the bookshop, looking for her mid-morning cup of coffee.

It had been a busy morning so far and Abby was feeling unusually weary. It was because she had so much playing on her mind, she thought, but she perked up a bit when she saw her friend.

'Hi,' she said, reaching for a coffee mug. 'I think I'll join you.'

'Why not?' Lori, a slim, attractive woman in her early thirties, grinned and propped her elbows on the counter. 'It seems pretty quiet at present.'

'It is now,' agreed Abby, filling the cups. 'How about a banana muffin?'

'You took the words right out of my mouth,' said Lori, sniffing appreciatively. 'You know, if I worked in here all day, I'd spend most of my time sampling the merchandise.' She grimaced. 'I'd soon be as fat as butter.'

'Not you,' said Abby, setting the muffin on a plate, adding a dessert fork, and handing it over. 'There you go. Enjoy.'

'I will.' Lori forked a mouthful of the muffin as Abby sipped her cappuccino, her expression mirroring her delight.

'This is awesome!'

'I'm glad you like it. It's a new recipe I found—'

The sudden surge of nausea took Abby completely by surprise. She felt the hot, strong beverage she'd been sipping rise into the back of her throat, and gagged. Then, lifting an apologetic hand towards Lori, she almost ran into the small bathroom situated at the back of the storage area.

Once again, she was violently sick. She had little in her stomach, but that didn't stop her from retching painfully. She was sluicing her face with cold water from the hand basin when Lori tapped on the open door.

'Hey, Abby,' she said, viewing her friend with some concern. 'Are you okay?'

Abby wiped her face with a tissue and turned with a shaky smile. 'I am now,' she said ruefully. 'Sorry.'

'Don't apologise.' Lori came to put an arm about her shoulders. 'Does this happen often?'

'Just today,' said Abby, resting her hips against the basin for support. 'I mean, I've felt a bit queasy for the past few days, but it's only today that I've actually thrown up.'

'So what do you think it is?'

Abby shrugged. 'I don't know. Something I've eaten, perhaps.' She paused. 'Do you think I should close the café?'

'That depends.' Lori straightened away from her. 'Have you eaten anything dodgy recently?'

'Well—no. Not that I can think of, anyway.'

Lori caught her lower lip between her teeth. 'Don't take this the wrong way, but you couldn't be pregnant, could you?' she asked awkwardly.

'You have been looking a bit—well—peaky for a couple of weeks.'

Abby stared at her in alarm. 'Pregnant?' she echoed. 'I—no. Of course not.'

Lori shifted uneasily from one foot to the other. 'But you have been seeing that guy who's bought Gifford's estate, haven't you? Luke Morelli. I recognised him the first time he came into the café weeks ago.' She grimaced. 'Blame it on the gossip magazines. I've seen his picture several times. He's usually escorting some glamorous socialite or other to a charity function or a film premiere. You know what men like him are like.'

Just the thought of that made Abby feel sick all over again.

'He's quite famous, you know.'

'Is he?' This was a side of Luke she'd never seen. But then, how well did she really know him? Not that well at all, it seemed.

There were a few tense moments when Abby just stared at her. Then she said cautiously, 'But how did you know I've been seeing him?' and Lori sighed.

'Greg told me,' she admitted. 'He's such an old gossip. I wouldn't have believed him, but Joan Miller said she'd seen Morelli's car outside the café one evening a few weeks ago, when she was going to see her sister.'

Abby licked her dry lips. 'He did call in, yes,' she conceded with some embarrassment. And then, because something more was needed, she added, 'I admit, I knew him before I came here, Lori. I met him—oh, years ago in London. When—when I was still married to my ex.'

'Hey, it's nothing to do with me,' exclaimed Lori, evidently regretting saying anything. 'And your being sick is probably just a bug. It's that time of year.'

'Yes.'

But Lori didn't sound convinced, and nor was Abby.

Then, after a moment, the other woman added, 'Perhaps I should tell you that Greg thinks you're using your influence with Luke Morelli to get the development cancelled.'

'What?'

Lori nodded. 'He says that's why you've been seeing him. That if anybody can change Morelli's mind, it's you.'

CHAPTER ELEVEN

ANGELICA RYAN, Luke's secretary, was waiting for him when he got to the office. Usually calm and efficient, today she was looking decidedly concerned.

She'd phoned Luke earlier in the morning to inform him there was a personal letter waiting for him at the office. She'd explained it was marked 'Private and Confidential' and that it had been posted in Bath.

Luke, who hadn't been planning on coming to Canary Wharf today, had decided to come and collect it. The alternative was to have a courier bring it to his house, but he'd abandoned that thought. It concerned him that it might be from his father's doctor and he'd rather not trust the letter to anyone else.

The last time he'd seen Oliver Morelli, he'd been grumbling about the pain in his shoulder. And, although his doctor had assured him it was nothing serious, Luke knew his grandfather had suffered from angina, and that his father was afraid he was developing the same complaint.

The envelope had no distinguishing marks, however, which was a relief. In fact, it didn't look like an official letter at all. But who would write to him here? Who did he know who might mark a letter 'Private and Confidential'? If it was a personal letter, why hadn't it been sent to his home address?

Going into his office, he seated himself at his desk and reached for a paper knife.

'Can I get you anything, Mr Morelli?'

Angelica was hovering in the doorway, evidently curious to know what it was. But Luke shook his head.

'Nothing, thanks,' he said, pausing until she'd got the message and closed the door behind her. Then, he slit the envelope open and drew out the slip of paper inside.

Abby was on the point of closing the café.

There were only two other people on the premises and they were in the bookshop. She could hear Lori talking to them, discussing the latest bestseller. Lori was the ideal saleswoman, as she was such an avid reader herself.

When the outer door opened, Abby stiffened instinctively.

But then, she'd been on tenterhooks for the

past two days. Ever since she'd sent that letter to the only address she could find for Luke, she'd been anticipating his arrival. Knowing him, as she did, she'd been sure he wouldn't trust any response to the phone.

And when she turned, she saw that it was indeed Luke.

He was dressed casually in jeans, with a dark green suede jacket hooked by a finger over one shoulder. He was also wearing a plain black tee, that couldn't help but emphasise the powerful muscles in his chest and arms.

He looked hot, she thought tensely, and she didn't mean his temperature.

'Hi,' he said, pausing just inside the door, and Abby was instantly aware of the sudden silence in the bookshop.

'Hi,' she said in response, glancing apprehensively towards that part of the premises. She was fairly sure that Lori had heard their voices and would presently appear.

Smoothing nervous hands over her hips, she glanced down at the hem of her short skirt. She should have been wearing something longer, she thought impatiently. The last thing she wanted was for Luke to think she wanted to pursue their relationship.

But she couldn't stay behind the counter indefinitely, and she crossed quickly to the arched entrance to the bookshop. As she'd half expected, she met Lori coming towards her.

Moistening her lips, she said, 'I'm going upstairs, Lori. Will you lock up when you're finished?'

'No problem,' said Lori, not without giving Luke a speculative glance. 'See you in the morning.'

'Yes.'

Abby nodded and then beckoned Luke to follow her up the stairs at the back of the serving area.

Harley met them at the door. The retriever was waiting to go out. Abby usually took him for a walk at this time of the day, but he was somewhat mollified when he saw Luke.

Luke bent to scratch the dog's ears and Abby moved past them into the small kitchenette that adjoined the main room. She was nervous. She couldn't deny it. But she didn't regret sending the letter, she assured herself. Not at all.

'Coffee? Tea?' she offered, reaching for the kettle, and Luke dropped his jacket onto the back of the sofa.

Did he give the tumbled cushions on the sofa a longer appraisal, or was that only her imagination? Was he remembering, as she was, exactly what had happened there some weeks ago?

From his enigmatic expression, she doubted it. Had he ever intended to contact her again?

Luke came to stand on the other side of the breakfast bar, and she felt her stomach muscles tighten. But all he said was, 'I'm assuming this isn't a social call.' He arched a brow inquiringly. 'What's happened? Has Hughes had a positive response to his petition?'

Abby's lips parted. 'You really think I'd tell you if he had?'

'Well, I can't think of any other reason for inviting me here,' he retorted shortly, and she shook her head in disbelief.

'I gather from your remarks that you didn't intend to come back,' she said, trying to control her indignation.

She had been such a fool where this man was concerned. Well, now she was going to pay for it, but she'd be damned before she'd let him have it all his own way.

Luke's eyes narrowed. 'Did you expect me to?' he remarked half mockingly now. 'Oh, Abby, I'm not denying you're a beautiful woman. Or that I wanted to have sex with you. I did. I still do. But I did warn you, I don't do commitment. And particularly not to a woman I can't trust.'

The arrogance of his remarks left her speechless for a moment.

Then, gathering herself, she said coldly, 'You

know nothing about me, Morelli. And even less about my life!'

'I know you cheated on your husband,' retorted Luke at once. 'I didn't like the bastard, but, God knows, he didn't deserve to be made to look a fool.'

'You think?' Abby was incensed. 'You don't know the first thing about Harry Laurence. Like all men, you think the woman must be to blame. He was a bastard. I agree with you on that. But don't underestimate your own abilities. When it comes to being a bastard, you've made the team.'

Luke scowled. 'If the only reason you've brought me here is to insult me—'

'It's not.' Abby swallowed convulsively. This wasn't how she'd hoped to tell him, but he wasn't giving her any choice. 'I'm pregnant, Morelli,' she said coldly. 'And before you ask the question, it's yours.'

Luke felt as if he'd just been punched in the gut.

It couldn't be true, he thought incredulously. He always took precautions. He never had sex without wearing a condom.

Apart from anything else, he'd never wanted to find himself in this position. Even when he was married to Sonia, he'd made sure there would be no unwanted babies.

Had he known even then that their marriage

was unlikely to last? Much as he'd wanted to deny it, Abby Laurence—Lacey—had ruined him for anyone else.

So how the hell...?

And then he remembered the first occasion he'd come to the apartment. It had been raining and he'd been virtually soaked to his skin. Abby had been straight out of the shower, all soft and warm and fragrant, and, stupidly, he'd lost his head.

God!

He stared at her, cupping the back of his neck with both hands and trying to get a handle on his emotions.

He was shocked; who wouldn't be shocked in the circumstances? But it was more than that. The realisation that he was going to be a father had stunned him. This girl—this girl he'd fought against caring about for so long—was going to have his child.

Abby's cheeks were flushed now and, although she was still wearing that belligerent expression, he realised what it must have cost her to blurt out a thing like that.

Particularly to someone who had just insulted her.

'Well?' she said, and he could see she was nervous. 'Aren't you going to call me a liar? After all, you've just said you can't trust me.'

Luke shook his head. 'How long have you known?'

Abby shrugged. 'I bought two testing kits a week ago. They were both positive.' She was trying to sound indifferent and failing abysmally. 'What can I say?'

'And—and how far along are you?'

She stiffened. 'I'm not having a termination.'

'Did I ask you to?' Luke spoke tersely and then lifted a hand, palm outward, to mitigate his words. 'I just meant—do you know how many weeks—?'

'Well, let me see.' She was sardonic. 'The first time we slept together was about five—six weeks ago. So I guess that sounds about right.'

Luke shook his head. 'Unbelievable.'

'What?' She looked contemptuously at him. 'I didn't want this, you know.' She paused. 'But—when a friend discovered what had happened, she insisted that I ought to tell—the father.'

Luke stared at her for a moment longer and then he said flatly, 'You know, I think I could do with that cup of tea now. Do you mind?'

Abby shrugged, but she turned back to the kettle she had been filling and set it on the ring. Then, taking down two cups from the shelf, she dropped a teabag in each.

'Sugar?' she asked, glancing briefly up at him, and Luke nodded.

'Two spoons, please,' he said, and then turned and made his way back to the sofa where he'd left his jacket.

Sitting down, he closed his eyes and raked back his hair with hands that weren't quite steady. Dear God, he'd never expected this. Abby was having a baby. She was having *his* baby. He was going to be a father!

His hands dropped between his spread knees and he took a deep breath, trying to steady himself. A damp nose nuzzling his palms was surprisingly comforting. Harley was now gazing up at him with his warm dark eyes, and he realised the dog had sensed something was wrong.

'Hey, boy,' he said, trying to get his head around what had happened. He managed a rueful grin. 'What are you going to do when there's a baby in the house?'

'That won't be your concern,' said Abby shortly, coming to set his cup on the low table in front of the sofa. 'Drink your tea while it's hot.'

Luke glanced up into her set face. Then he patted the sofa beside him. 'Sit down, Abby. We need to talk.'

Abby regarded him coolly for a few moments, then she collected her tea from the breakfast bar and seated herself in the armchair at right angles to the sofa.

'There's not a lot more to be said,' she declared. 'I've done my duty. You know the score. And when the baby's born, I won't stop you from seeing him—or her—if that's what you want.'

'Hold up.' Luke, who had taken a couple of mouthfuls of his tea, now set his cup back on the table. 'Let's not get ahead of ourselves here. Since when have I said that you and our child will be living apart from me?'

Abby caught her breath, trying to pull that absurdly short skirt over her knees. 'It's not your decision to make. And I hope you're not implying what I think you're implying.'

'And that would be?'

'That we live together.'

'Why not?'

The words were out before Luke could stop them, but they didn't have the anticipated effect.

She shook her head. 'Oh, no, Morelli. You don't get to call the shots here. You said it yourself, you don't do commitment. And I have no intention of putting my baby—'

'*Our* baby!'

'—at the mercy of your casual liaisons with other women.'

Luke got angrily to his feet. 'What right have you to accuse me of having casual liaisons?'

Abby rose, too, though he noticed she stepped away from him before replying. 'Well, what was this?' she demanded, spreading a hand to encompass the apartment. 'You had no intention of seeing me again. You've just admitted as much.'

'I didn't say that.' Luke's jaw was clenched so tight, he could feel the pulse racing beneath his ear. 'In any case, that was—before,' he said inadequately, and Abby gave a short laugh.

'Before I'd trapped you, is that it?' She lifted her chin. 'Well, I've got news for you, Morelli—'

'Stop calling me Morelli!'

'—I've got no intention of trapping you. Or of living with you, for that matter. This is the twenty-first century, Luke. Women don't need to rely on men to support them. Right now, I've got the café, and when that closes, I'll find a job. Or other premises, who knows? Whatever, you won't be involved.'

Luke's frustration knew no bounds. 'You can't stop me from being involved.'

'Oh, I think I can.' She lifted her hands to release her hair from its ponytail. 'There's no law that says I have to do anything more than I've already done. You know about the baby now.

And after it's born, you'll have your chance to share custody or not. That's up to you.'

Luke scowled. He knew she was right, but that didn't stop him from resenting the ultimatum she'd given him. And while he had said the things she'd accused him of, the truth was he had wanted to see her again, damn her.

'I need to think about this,' he muttered, aware that she had never looked more desirable than she did at that moment.

He'd always admired her legs and the short skirt showed them to perfection. Add to that the sleeveless vest that outlined the pert fullness of her breasts, and exposed the moist hollow between, and he was fascinated. A pearl of perspiration invited him to taste, and he could already feel his erection tightening his jeans painfully across his crotch.

'Abby...' he began roughly, but she was already walking towards the door.

'I think you'd better go,' she said, without a trace of expression in her voice. 'Thank you for coming. Goodbye.'

Luke followed her across the room, but when she stepped aside to allow him to leave, his hand hit the wall beside her head, backing her up until there was scarcely a breath between them.

'This isn't over, Abby,' he said harshly, his

mouth hot against her neck, and he heard her catch an unsteady breath.

'It is,' she insisted, her voice barely audible as she pressed him away from her. 'Just go, Luke. I wish I never had to see you again.'

CHAPTER TWELVE

DURING THE FOLLOWING WEEKS, Luke focused on his work to the exclusion of everything else.

He spent more time in the office than he had done for years, even if his staff didn't appreciate having him on their backs every minute of the day.

But it was only at work that he could escape the torment of his thoughts.

Since leaving Abby at her flat, he'd done everything he could to get what she had told him into some kind of perspective.

He knew his life would never be the same again. That was a given. And the shock he'd experienced at her news had made him speak without considering his words. But, dammit all, he was only human. He was just afraid he'd blown any connection he might have had with her big time.

And why did he care so much? He kept reminding himself of what she'd done to Harry

Laurence. For God's sake, he had only her word that she was pregnant. She could have made the whole thing up to see what his reaction would be.

But in his heart of hearts he knew that wasn't true. As much as he might tell himself that he despised the way she'd treated her husband, he sensed there was an element of truth in everything she'd said.

Which meant what? That Harry Laurence had been no saint, and Luke had jumped to the wrong conclusion? She'd tried to tell him why she'd done what she had, but he'd never been prepared to listen to her.

Nonetheless, she had lied to her husband when she'd come to meet him. And nothing could alter the fact that she'd remained Laurence's wife for at least a year after those events. Surely, if Laurence had been as bad as she'd said he was, she would have got a divorce.

Maybe it was simply that she'd enjoyed the luxury of being a pampered wife, he speculated bitterly. She wouldn't be the first woman who'd wanted to have her cake and eat it, too.

He'd met a number of women like that, when he'd been obliged to enter the social circuit. Or should he say 'circus', he amended wryly, mocking the concept. He had to admit that that was one aspect of being a successful entrepreneur that he didn't enjoy.

He scowled down at the plans he'd been studying, and wondered what Harry Laurence was doing these days. He'd heard that he'd left the Stock Exchange soon after his divorce.

At the time, Luke had assumed that Harry had wanted a fresh start. That it might have been hard for him to face his colleagues after such a personal defeat.

It might be interesting to find out why Abby's husband had sued for a divorce. If it *was* Laurence who had done so. He couldn't believe Abby had made a habit of having extra-marital affairs. She didn't seem the type. Although, in all honesty, he didn't know why.

Still, there was no way of finding out what had happened now. He knew no one who had been a friend of Abby's at that time. Had there been someone she'd confided in? Someone who knew why the marriage had broken down?

It was a problem that occupied his mind for the next few days. An unnecessary problem, he conceded, but at least it took his mind from other things.

Like what Abby was doing now. Had she meant what she'd said when she'd insisted she wouldn't have a termination? Ironic as it seemed in the present circumstances, Luke didn't want her to lose the child either.

His child!

Their child!

Of all the people in his life, it was Felix who noticed Luke's preoccupation. The two men had been close since they were in the army, and, despite the difference in their circumstances these days, Felix had always felt able to speak his mind.

Driving his employer home from a meeting in Oxford some days later, he remarked casually, 'Have you made any plans about when you're going to deal with those shops in Ashford-St-James? You said there was some sort of petition going round. Did that come to anything, or shouldn't I ask?'

Luke, who had been studying his laptop in the back of the Bentley, now lifted his head. 'According to our solicitors, they don't stand a chance of halting the development. But I have given the type of development it's going to be some thought.'

'Oh, yes?'

'Yes.' Luke hesitated, and then said, 'I'm having discussions at present with the architects, and we're seriously considering amending the plans.'

'Amending them?'

Felix sounded amused, and Luke gave him a warning look. 'Yeah, amending them,' he said shortly. 'To incorporate a small shopping mall that leads into the supermarket proper. The shops in the mall would be rented, of course. Perhaps some of the tenants from South Road would be interested.'

'Perhaps they would.' Felix met Luke's eyes in the rear-view mirror and arched a brow. 'Maybe even a certain café-cum-bookstore owner?' he offered ingenuously. 'I'm sure it would be a great relief to her and all the other tenants.'

Luke scowled. 'Don't look so smug. It's not a done deal yet.'

'But it will be,' said Felix assuredly. 'I liked—Abby. That is what you called her, isn't it? She was certainly a looker. And nice with it, as well.'

'Looks aren't everything,' muttered Luke broodingly, and Felix inclined his head in agreement. 'In any case,' Luke continued, 'I'm not doing this just for Abby Lacey.'

'Of course not.'

But Felix didn't sound convinced, and who could blame him? Luke didn't believe it himself.

Tossing and turning in bed that night—not an unusual occurrence these days—Luke was forced to admit that he *was* doing it for Abby. Despite everything that had happened, despite the fact that she'd said she wanted nothing more to do with him, he couldn't accept it. He wouldn't accept it.

He cared about her, dammit. He suspected he always had.

Okay, maybe she'd acted selfishly in the past; and maybe she'd had some justification, as she'd claimed. Whatever the truth of the matter was, he wanted to see her again. He wanted to be with her. He loved her. And he'd never felt like that about any woman before.

Unable to sleep any longer with that scenario buzzing around in his head, Luke got up and went downstairs to make himself some coffee. And found Felix, sitting in the kitchen, drinking tea and getting a march on the morning's newspapers.

Mrs Webb was there, too, gossiping away about the latest episode of her favourite soap. But he doubted Felix had heard a word of it. He was too busy absorbing what he'd found in the *Daily Globe*.

'Oh, Luke!' Mrs Webb gazed at him in surprise, and even Felix put the newspaper aside with an apologetic grin. 'You're an early riser. It's barely half past six. Is something wrong?'

'What could be wrong, Mrs Webb?' Luke walked across to the cooker and helped himself to a mug of coffee. 'I couldn't sleep, that's all. I thought I'd get an early start.'

'An early start?'

It was Felix who echoed his words, and Luke nodded. 'Yes. I'm driving down to Ashford this morning. And I'm sure the roads will be busy with holiday traffic, so the sooner I start, the better.'

Felix slid off his stool. 'I'll get the car.'

'No, there's no need, Felix. I'm going to drive myself.'

Felix frowned. 'You sure?'

'I'm sure.' Luke gave him a wry look. 'You can have the day off. Go and visit that daughter of yours.'

Felix had had a brief liaison before he'd gone into the army and his daughter was the result. And despite the fact that he'd never married her mother, he and his daughter were surprisingly close.

'She's away,' said Felix glumly. 'She and her boyfriend are in Majorca, enjoying the sun.'

'Oh.' Luke considered. 'Well—do something else then.

'I tell you what: try and find out what a guy called Harry Laurence is doing these days.'

Abby had had her first trip to see her doctor that morning.

She'd decided to close the café for the day, as

Lori couldn't cope with the morning rush and attend to the bookstore at the same time.

Still, as she walked back to South Road she was feeling pretty good, and she was wondering whether she should open up that afternoon. It would mean contacting Lori, but, as it was a pretty miserable day, she didn't think her friend would mind.

Everything changed when she saw the car, parked illegally, across the road from the café.

She didn't recognise it, but it was an expensive vehicle.

An Aston Martin, if she wasn't mistaken. The type of car Luke had driven years ago. And although she wanted to remain calm and collected, her pulse started racing madly.

If it was Luke, what was he doing here? Had he come to give her and the other shopkeepers their notices to quit? If so, she might have less than six months to find another home and another job. And not just for her, she acknowledged anxiously. In less than seven months, she would need a home for her baby, as well.

Almost instinctively, she ran a hand over her stomach.

Was it only her imagination, or could she feel a slight mound beneath her shirt?

She was over eight weeks now and the doctor

had said that in another two weeks, she should have her first ultrasound scan. The idea of being able to see the baby inside her was tantalising. To have living proof her son or daughter was real.

Ought she to ask Luke if he wanted to go with her to the hospital? She didn't want to, but it was his baby, too. He was just as responsible for its existence as she was. And she had the feeling that he wouldn't refuse such an invitation if he could fit it into his busy life.

As she neared the car a door was thrust open and, as on that other occasion, a long jean-clad leg emerged. It was Luke, lean and dark, and endlessly appealing, in a black button-down shirt, and deck shoes.

To her surprise, he looked relieved to see her. And she guessed he'd already read the notice on the café door. Where did he think she'd been? she wondered. She was tempted to say she'd been looking for a new place to live. But she didn't want to start lying to him now.

He came across the road as she neared the café. 'Are you okay?' he asked, regarding her closely. 'When I saw the café was closed, I thought you must be ill.'

'Did you try the side door?' she asked, without answering his question. She could imagine the uproar Harley would have caused if he'd heard someone hammering on the door.

'I knocked,' agreed Luke, 'but when Harley started barking, I guessed you couldn't be there.'

'Or I'd have come rushing down to greet you?' suggested Abby drily, and Luke pulled a face.

'Uh, no,' he said defensively. 'But he wouldn't have continued barking if you'd been there to shut him up.'

Abby inclined her head, conceding the point. Then, glancing across at his car, she said, 'You'll get a parking ticket. The wardens are pretty active around here.'

'So I'll pay the fine,' said Luke indifferently. 'Or rather, Felix will. He handles all that sort of thing for me.'

Abby shook her head. 'So why are you here? Have you come to tell us when we have to leave? If so, I'll ask the other tenants—'

'I'm not here to ask anyone to leave,' retorted Luke between his teeth. He paused. 'I wanted to see you.'

'Why?'

'Do I have to have a reason?' He sighed. 'Let's go inside and we can talk.'

Abby looked up at him, despising herself for the way her stomach clenched at the sight of him. Why was he really here? It could only be about the baby. She tensed at the thought that he might be considering trying to take over the child's life as soon as it was born.

Surely even Luke would not be that cruel. Though his careless comments about parking his car proved that abiding by the rules meant little to him.

But she had to find out, one way or the other, and, with a shrug, she walked past him into the alley beside the café.

She was conscious of him following her, of his powerful body behind hers as she unlocked the door and stepped inside. But, before she could even close the door, he backed her up against the wall in the hall and gripped the back of her neck, tipping her face up to his.

His mouth was hot and demanding, and she was incapable of resisting him. Desire shivered through her, and, although he was supporting himself with his free hand so he wouldn't crush her, Abby felt the unmistakeable thrust of his powerful arousal against her abdomen.

'I've been worried sick about you,' he muttered, cupping her face with his hands, his thumbs brushing her parted lips. 'Where the hell have you been?'

Abby was breathless. 'Why do you care?'

'Because I do, all right?' He kissed her again, this time giving in to the urge to push himself against her. 'I've been waiting for the better part of an hour. I've even had to pacify a few of your customers, who turned up expecting their morning fix.'

His hands curved down her spine to her hips, lifting her until his sex fitted neatly into the hollow between her legs. 'I want you, Abby. I don't know how I've stayed away.'

'Because I asked you to.'

Somehow, Abby managed to slide out from between him and the wall and slam the open door. She could imagine Greg Hughes' reaction if he'd passed by as Luke was kissing her.

Turning back to her visitor, who was now unwillingly leaning back against the wall, she said quietly, 'I've been to see the doctor. Why didn't you ring before you left London? I could have told you not to come.'

Then she hurried away upstairs. Harley had started barking again, and she didn't want him to attract any more attention, not with Luke's car parked significantly across the street.

Or that was her excuse.

The truth was, she was too vulnerable at the moment. Whether it was her hormones, or simply the knowledge that she loved this man, whatever his faults, she didn't trust herself not to say or do something she would later regret.

In consequence, she had to keep him at arm's length, however impossible that might prove to be.

CHAPTER THIRTEEN

LUKE MANAGED TO calm the retriever's exuberant welcome, and, putting the dog aside, he looked at Abby.

She was wearing a loose shirt and shorts today, the hem of the shorts exposing surprisingly tanned legs. And she looked incredible to his hungry eyes.

God, he wanted to touch her again.

But he had to consider her feelings.

'You've been to see the doctor?' he said, his nerves tightening. 'Why? Is something wrong?'

She gave him a disbelieving look. 'Hello? I'm pregnant. In case you've forgotten.'

'Yeah, right. Like I'm going to forget something like that.' Luke spoke tersely. 'But you're okay?'

'I'm fine.' He noticed she'd put the width of the breakfast bar between them as he was soothing the retriever. 'Do you want a drink? I have some cola in the fridge.'

'I'm not thirsty.' Luke sucked in a breath. 'What did the doctor say exactly?'

Abby gasped. 'I don't remember *exactly* what he said.'

She moistened her lips and then continued, 'I'm over eight weeks pregnant. My blood pressure is good, and the nausea I suffered in the first few weeks has virtually gone.'

'I didn't know you'd suffered from nausea.'

'And that surprises you?'

Luke acknowledged the barb, raking back his hair with both hands as he started towards her. One of the buttons on his shirt popped as he lifted his arms, and he was ridiculously pleased to see the way her eyes went straight to the tuft of dark hair that could now be seen poking through the cloth.

But he had to be practical.

'Can we sit down? I want to talk to you.'

Abby stiffened. 'You sit down. I'm all right here.'

'But don't you think you should sit down? I guess you walked to the surgery, so you've probably been on your feet for quite some time.'

Abby's mouth turned down. 'Being pregnant doesn't make me an invalid, Luke.'

'I know.' He was reassured that she hadn't used his surname as she'd done the last time he was here. 'But—humour me. I'm only think-ing of you.'

'And that's a first,' she remarked tightly. 'What do you want, Luke? If it's not about the café, it must be about the baby.'

Luke sighed. 'Sit down. Please.'

'Oh, all right.'

With evident reluctance, she came out from behind the breakfast bar. Meanwhile Luke had deliberately positioned himself in front of the armchair she'd used on that other occasion. And when he indicated the sofa, she had no choice but to perch on one end.

Of course, he seated himself beside her, and saw the way she pressed herself against the arm to avoid touching him. But, however she be-haved, whatever she said, she wasn't indifferent to him. He'd proved it downstairs. He just had to persuade her he wasn't the unfeeling bastard she thought he was.

He was sitting staring at her, when she said testily, 'Can we get on with this? Why are you here?' She paused. 'I'm not going to have sex with you again.'

'Well, not now, perhaps,' remarked Luke drily, and her face suffused with colour at his words.

'Not ever,' she retorted coldly. Then, as if realising what he was thinking, she added, 'Not willingly, anyway.'

Luke stiffened now. 'I hope you're not implying that I've ever forced you.'

Abby sighed. 'N-o-o,' she admitted, dragging the word out. 'I was as much to blame.'

'To blame?' he echoed. 'There was no blame, Abby. I wanted you. I still do.' He paused. 'But I guess you know that.'

Abby's eyes darted to his, then away again. 'Then you want what you can't have,' she said quietly. 'I know what you think of me, Luke. You've made that perfectly clear.'

Luke blew out a breath, stretching out his hand towards her. But when he would have touched her knee, she shifted away.

'Abby,' he said cajolingly, 'I know I've made some mistakes in the past. A whole lot of them. But I want you to give me a chance to make amends.'

'How?' She spoke bitterly. 'You still think I betrayed Harry by agreeing to meet you.'

'That was nearly six years ago,' he protested. 'Maybe I was too willing to jump to the wrong conclusion. Let's face it, I didn't know Laurence from Adam—'

'No, you didn't.'

'—and he could have been the biggest jerk in

Christendom. You might have had some justification for doing what you did.'

'Might have?' Abby gave a mirthless laugh. 'Oh, Luke, you don't know the half of it.'

'So tell me.'

'Why?'

'Because I want to know. I want to know everything there is to know about you.'

'Why?' she demanded again, and then pushed herself up from the sofa with an angry gesture. 'No, don't bother answering that. I know why. This is because of the baby, isn't it?' Her lips twisted. 'You're afraid that if we're not on speaking terms when the baby's born, I'll conduct the same kind of vendetta against you that you've conducted against me.'

Luke shot up from the sofa, startling Harley, who had been lying on the rug at his feet. 'The hell I am,' he muttered, his eyes dark with emotion. 'I want you to know how I feel about you, that's all. I've been a fool. I realise that. But can't you see, I've learned my lesson?'

Abby shook her head. 'It's too late, Luke. I don't believe your protestations of regret, any more than you believed mine.'

She held up her head. 'I think you ought to go. You've done your duty and assured yourself that there are no complications thus far. But after this, I suggest you send Felix if you want an update on my condition.'

Luke hooked one hand behind his neck. 'That's not why I came,' he said roughly. 'Sure, I've wondered how you were, but you've got no idea how many times I've picked up the phone and put it down again.'

'To call your broker, no doubt,' she said contemptuously, and this time she achieved her objective. He was furious.

'No, not to call my broker,' he snarled angrily. 'For God's sake, Abby, what do you want me to do? Get down on my knees and beg you to believe me? If I thought it would do any good, I'd do it. I love you, dammit. And I've never said that to any woman before.'

Abby's lips parted, and she backed away from him. 'My God,' she said disbelievingly, 'you'll do anything to own this baby, won't you?'

Luke could only stare at her. 'Is that what you think?' His voice broke on the words. 'Well, yeah, if that's what you believe, you're right. I am wasting my time.'

'I told you that,' she said, but now she was looking and sounding a little less than self-assured.

Or was that only wishful thinking? Certainly, when he moved towards her, she flinched away from him as if he were about to attack her.

His eyes narrowed. Was it conceivable that that was how Laurence had treated her? Recalling the bruise he'd seen on her neck that fateful evening, it was possible.

He felt sick suddenly. 'Abby,' he began in a gentler tone, but she turned away from him.

'Go,' she said, her voice thick with emotion, but Luke couldn't just walk out.

Catching her arm, he swung her round to face him, not surprised to find the evidence of unshed tears in her eyes.

'Abby,' he said again, and, unable to prevent himself, he bent and pressed a warm kiss to the corner of her soft mouth. 'I do love you,' he added huskily. And without waiting to see if she would say anything else to defend herself, he strode across the room and ran down the stairs before he could change his mind.

But he'd be back, he assured himself as he slammed the outer door behind him. She could bet on it.

It was late in the evening when Abby heard someone knocking at her door.

Of course, Harley started barking, and she sighed in frustration.

But her pulse quickened in spite of herself. It could only be Luke, she thought tensely. It was after eleven and no one else was likely to turn up at this hour. And she knew exactly what he wanted.

It was annoying because she'd spent the rest of the day trying to put what he'd said out of her mind. She hadn't even had her work in the café to distract her. There'd been no point in opening in the middle of the afternoon, and by the time Luke had gone, she'd been in no state to face her customers, anyway.

She'd suspected he'd come back, of course, only not so precipitately. Certainly not just a few hours after he'd left. It was as she'd said: he wanted to maintain a connection with her so that when the baby was born, she wouldn't be able to deny him access to the child.

There was no doubt that finding out he was going to be a father had shocked him. For heaven's sake, it had shocked her, and she'd at least had some warning of what was happening to her body.

She bit her lip. He probably thought at this time of the evening, she'd be more responsive to his persuasion; more willing to believe his protestations of love.

Love? Her lips twisted. No way.

Harley was growling now, pacing back and forth before the door that led onto the stairs, and she felt a moment's apprehension.

What if it wasn't Luke? The dog wasn't usually suspicious of Luke, but surely even the retriever couldn't detect a person's scent from so far away.

She hesitated, glancing down at the silk kimono she was wearing over her nightshirt. She certainly wasn't dressed for company, but then who else would turn up without even a word of warning?

It had to be Luke, and she had to send him away before Harley woke the whole street.

Opening the door, she switched on the light, and allowed the retriever to precede her down the stairs. He was still growling when he reached the bottom and she took a deep breath before calling stiffly, 'I'm not going to let you in, Luke. I'm sorry if you've had a wasted journey, but—'

'It's not Luke, Ms Lacey.' The man interrupted her, his voice oddly choked, but familiar. 'It's Felix. Felix Laidlaw. I work for Luke.' He paused. 'There's been an accident, Ms Lacey. Luke's been hurt and he's asking for you.' Another pause. 'Will you open the door?'

Abby's lips parted in dismay.

Her hands went automatically to the lock, but then she drew back, pressing the tips of her fingers to her lips. How did she know he was telling the truth?

There was no way of knowing, and the door was old, so it didn't have a spyhole.

'Ms Lacey? Abby?' Felix—if it was Felix—
spoke again. 'Please, I know you must be suspicious. But I'm not lying. Luke's in hospital.
In Bath.'

'In Bath!' Abby swallowed. 'I don't understand. What's Luke doing in Bath? I understood
he was going back to London.'

'He was, but he was going to see his father
first.' He sighed. 'Couldn't I tell you what happened when we're on our way? I need to get
back.'

Abby bit her lip. 'I'm not even dressed.'

'I'll wait.'

Abby hesitated. 'How do I know you're telling the truth?'

'You don't.' Felix's tone was flat now. 'But
are you prepared to let a man die, without even
trying to save him?'

Abby gasped, and, without any more hesitation, she had the door open in seconds. As she'd
expected, Felix was outside, his face pale in the
light from the hall behind her.

'Luke's dying?' she choked, dragging Harley
back as he would have surged outside, and Felix
expelled a weary breath.

'Not yet,' he said honestly. 'But he's badly
hurt.'

'Hurt? How?'

'His car was in collision with a farm vehicle,'

replied Felix heavily. 'The fool driver of the combine harvester pulled into the road right in front of him. It's lucky he wasn't killed outright. Now, can you get dressed and come with me?'

'Oh, God!'

Abby didn't say another word. Leaving the retriever to his own devices, she turned and raced back up the stairs, hurrying into the bathroom. She was feeling sick again, but she couldn't consider her own condition now.

She didn't hesitate and tore off her kimono and nightshirt and pulled on the shirt and shorts, not bothering with any underwear.

By the time she emerged from the bathroom, both Harley and Felix were waiting for her in the living room.

'I hope you don't mind.' Felix was apologetic. 'But your dog was threatening to run off, so I brought him inside.'

'That's fine. Thank you.' Abby moistened her lips. 'I'm ready.'

'You'll need a sweater,' said Felix gently. 'It's cold outside.'

'I'm fine, honestly.'

Abby thought she'd never feel cold again, and, with a resigned gesture, Felix started for the door.

CHAPTER FOURTEEN

LUKE OPENED HIS eyes to a blinding white light, and quickly closed them again.

His head was throbbing, and he could hear the hum of what sounded like electrical instruments all around him. The steady drip of liquid was almost deafening to his ears.

He risked opening his eyes again and saw the strip of neon in the ceiling above him. That was what was blinding him.

Why didn't they turn the damn thing off?

Was he in a hospital? The pain of applying his brain almost caused him to lose consciousness again. But if he was, how the hell had he got here? He didn't remember a thing after getting into his car.

The smell of Lysol and pine disinfectant was sickening and he gagged. His mouth was so dry, he felt as if all his saliva glands had given up in protest.

There was a man standing beside his bed,

when he opened his eyes again. He didn't think it was a doctor. Doctors were supposed to wear white coats, weren't they? Unless they'd taken to wearing worn canvas trousers and sweaters. Anything was possible in this surreal world he was existing in.

His eyes drifted upward to the man's face, and he expelled a relieved breath. He recognised him.

It was his father. But what was his father doing here? Oliver Morelli's face looked strained and anxious, but so familiar Luke wanted to reach out and touch him.

But he couldn't move.

When he tried, an agonising pain knifed into his ribs, and he couldn't deny a groan of anguish.

Oliver Morelli saw his son's eyes open and gave a cry of relief. 'Luke,' he exclaimed fervently. 'Oh, dear God, I've been so worried about you.'

Luke stared at him. He tried to say his father's name, but no sound emerged. His mouth was too dry, his lips too parched to form the words.

But Oliver Morelli didn't seem to notice. 'Do you remember anything of the last twenty-four hours?' he asked, pulling a chair out from beside the bed and dropping into it.

'You were conscious when they first brought you into the hospital, but then—'

He broke off as if he didn't want to say what had happened next, and when he continued, it was in a very different vein. 'How do you feel? Are you in pain? Can I get you anything?'

A drink?

Luke tried to speak, but all he produced was a guttural sound, and, looking alarmed, Oliver got to his feet again.

'I'll get the nurse,' he said, but somehow Luke managed to get a name past his lips.

'Ab—Abby,' he breathed hoarsely, and his father, who had hurried across the room, turned back from the door.

'Abby?' he said. 'Oh, you mean the young lady who was here when I arrived?'

Luke absorbed that with some difficulty. Abby had been here? But how? And where was she now?

Frustrated at his own helplessness, he was filled with a feeling of defeat. His head throbbed with the effort of trying to think. Once again, he attempted to speak, but before he could formulate the words a nurse bustled into the room.

She saw at once that the patient was conscious and she turned sharply to his father. 'How long has Mr Morelli been awake?' she asked, her tone reproving. 'You should have come and fetched me, as soon as he regained consciousness.'

'Minutes, only,' said Oliver apologetically. 'I was going to come and let you know, but—'

'It doesn't matter.'

The nurse came to look down at Luke with critical eyes. Then she gave her attention to something that was above his head; a screen, possibly. Turning, she checked another monitor that was ticking away beside him, making notes on a clipboard she'd taken from a slot at the bottom of his bed.

As his brain kicked in he realised that there were tubes and wires attached to various parts of his body. There was something in his nose and another tube going into his mouth. What had happened to him?

After assessing the contents of the drip that was attached to his arm, the nurse frowned. 'How are you feeling, Mr Morelli?' she asked, repeating his father's words. 'Do you remember how you got here?'

Luke's tongue pushed helplessly between his lips, and the woman nodded her understanding.

'You'd like a drink, yes?' She reached for a jug of water that Luke realised must have been sitting on the bedside table all the time and poured a small amount into a glass. Then, after attaching a straw, she held it to his lips. 'Just a little.'

The water was cool and delicious. Luke felt as if he could have drunk all that was in the glass and more. But after a few sips, the nurse drew it away.

'That will do for now, Mr Morelli. I'll get Mr Marsden.'

'No…'

Somehow Luke got the word out, but the nurse only shook her head. 'Mr Marsden asked to be informed as soon as you regained consciousness,' she said firmly.

Luke said nothing more. He was aware that for the present, his opinion meant nothing at all.

'Don't upset yourself, Mr Morelli,' the nurse continued briskly. 'Mr Marsden was the surgeon who dealt with your injuries when you first arrived at the hospital. He's taken a personal interest in your case, and I know he'll want to assess your condition for himself.'

She was out of the door before Luke could offer any further protest and as soon as she'd gone his father resumed his position beside the bed.

'Do you remember anything about the accident?' he asked anxiously.

And Luke, who had been wondering why he'd needed a surgeon in the first place, was suddenly thrust back to the moment when he'd realised the heavy farm vehicle, lumbering out of the field, wasn't going to stop.

The memory of what had happened slammed into him with the force of a freight train. His brain suddenly felt as if it were exploding, pain radiating to every part of his skull. Blood throbbed in his temples, and his heartbeat accelerated. He felt again the horror of what he'd had to face.

His eyes closed, and this time he didn't try to open them. He thought he heard his father utter a cry of protest. But all he could do was give in to the pain, and pray for blessed relief.

Abby sat in the waiting area attached to the intensive care unit of the hospital and wished she knew if Luke had regained consciousness yet.

She hoped so. Oh, God, she hoped so.

When she'd first seen him, she'd been horrified, sure that Felix hadn't been exaggerating when he'd said that Luke was in a critical condition after the accident.

He'd still been covered in blood when she'd been allowed to enter the trauma unit, and all she could do was pray that the paramedics, who had airlifted him to the hospital, had got to him in time.

And he had been conscious at that time, asking for Abby, as Felix had said. When she'd appeared at his bedside, he'd recognised her instantly, grasping her hand and bringing it to his lips.

'Love you,' he'd said, his voice barely recognisable. And Abby had turned her fingers until they were grasping his, uncaring that they were soon as covered in blood as his were.

'Oh, Luke,' she'd whispered brokenly, wishing there were something she could do to ease his pain. 'I love you, too.'

But he hadn't responded. The nurses in the trauma unit had already been telling her she must wait outside, and Abby had realised Luke hadn't heard a word she'd said. He'd lost consciousness the moment after he'd spoken those words to her.

Had he even known she was there? She didn't know, and no one had bothered to tell her. She'd just been shunted into the corridor and told to find the waiting area.

Her only comfort had been Felix, who had been pacing about the room where relatives and friends were expected to wait.

He'd seen her tear-stained face, and had immediately come to give her a hug. 'He'll make it,' he'd told her gruffly. 'Luke's a tough customer. No old combine harvester's going to beat him.'

'That's not what you said before,' Abby had reminded him, sniffing back her tears. 'Oh, Felix, I feel so responsible.'

'Why?'

Felix had been so sympathetic that she hadn't been able to stop herself from telling him about the row they'd had before Luke had left the apartment.

Somehow, she'd managed not to mention the baby. That was something Luke would have to tell him if—*when*—he recovered.

Of course, Felix had reassured her that she was blaming herself unnecessarily. As far as he knew, Luke hadn't been driving recklessly, as he might have been if he'd been in a bad frame of mind. He'd simply been going to see his father, before driving back to London.

'The accident could have happened to anyone,' he'd said gently. 'Try and relax. We may have some time to wait.'

Luke's father had arrived a few minutes later. He'd come into the waiting room looking dazed, and Felix had immediately gone to speak to him.

There'd been a whispered conversation, during which the older man had cast a questioning look in Abby's direction. She'd guessed he was asking who she was and Felix was telling him.

Then Felix had accompanied him along the corridor to the ICU.

Felix had eventually returned alone, and for the next few hours they'd sat mostly in silence, only exchanging an occasional word, each occupied with their own thoughts.

The following morning, a doctor—she didn't know his name—had come to inform them that Luke was in a coma. He'd said they shouldn't worry about it; that the doctors were doing all they could to relieve his pain. He'd said he would let them know as soon as the patient was conscious again.

Apparently unaware that Abby's face had lost all colour, he'd then suggested they should go home and get some rest. He'd said he'd phone them if there was any news.

Abby hadn't wanted to leave the hospital. She'd been afraid that something terrible might happen if she wasn't there.

But Felix had reminded her that she couldn't stay in the waiting room indefinitely. And Harley was at home, waiting to be fed.

But that had been three days ago now. And, although she'd gone through the motions of caring for Harley, putting notices out that the café would be closed for the foreseeable future, reassuring her neighbours that she wasn't ill, but that a close friend was, her heart had never been in it.

She'd phoned the hospital constantly. But, as she wasn't a close relative, their information had been impersonal at best. Felix had given her his number, thank goodness, and she'd been able to phone him for news. He'd proved a tower of strength, assuring her that Luke's condition hadn't deteriorated. That he was progressing as well as they could hope.

The coma, however frightening it sounded, was allowing his body to mend. He was receiving the very best treatment and everything that could be done for him was being done.

Which hadn't done a lot to improve Abby's sleeping habits.

When she'd slept at all, it had been fitful, filled with horrific dreams of Luke colliding with the huge farming machine.

It hadn't helped to hear from Felix that the driver of the combine harvester was being charged with dangerous driving. It didn't do anything to improve Luke's injuries, which even she, with her limited knowledge, had realised must be very serious indeed.

So she'd come back to the hospital, hoping that, as she was there, she might be allowed to see the patient. But so far, she'd had no success. The nurses were polite but firm, and she didn't have Felix to turn to because he was attending to other matters. She hadn't even been allowed a glimpse of Luke through the windows of the ICU.

A man appeared in the waiting-room doorway at that moment and she realised it was Luke's father. She hadn't seen him since that first night at the hospital, when he'd turned up looking as if he'd just got out of bed.

She'd probably looked the same, she conceded, remembering her panic when Felix had come to fetch her. But she'd had more time to attend to her appearance today, and so had he.

He looked at her consideringly for a moment, and then said, 'It's Abby, isn't it? Felix didn't introduce us, but he tells me Luke asked for you. I'm Oliver Morelli. Luke's father.'

Abby rose to her feet, her heartbeat quickening at the memory of Luke's choked words. 'Yes,' she said, shaking the hand he held out to her. She paused. 'This must have been a terrible shock for you. It's been a terrible shock for all of us.'

'Yes.' Judging by the haggard lines around the older man's eyes, he wasn't sleeping very well either. He frowned. 'Have you seen Luke this morning?'

'I haven't seen him since the night he was

brought into the hospital,' she admitted. 'I'm not a relative, you see. Just—just a concerned friend.'

'Really?' Oliver Morelli frowned. 'Don't you own one of the businesses in South Road?'

'Well, yes—'

'Oh, dear.' Oliver grimaced. 'I seem to remember that Luke told me the tenants had organised a petition against that development. I'm sure he could do without any more stress now.'

'I had nothing to do with the petition,' said Abby defensively. 'And I'm certainly not here because Luke plans to develop the site where my café stands.'

Oliver shook his head. 'Oh, well, I suppose that's something,' he said. And then, rather sadly, 'I doubt if Luke even remembers the development at present. I must go and speak to his doctor. Marsden said he might have some news for me today.'

Abby caught her breath. 'Could I come with you?'

Oliver Morelli looked doubtful, and she was sure he was about to refuse.

But then his expression changed. 'Well, he did ask for you again, on the one occasion he regained consciousness,' he admitted, shocking her completely. 'You didn't know that?' This because she swayed on her feet and he reached out to save her. 'Oh, yes, yours was the first name on his lips when he opened his eyes.'

He helped her regain her balance, and then added ruefully, 'Unfortunately, he lost consciousness again soon after.'

CHAPTER FIFTEEN

THE SUITE OF rooms Luke was occupying was as tastefully furnished as the rest of the house.

The sitting area was large, with lots of flowers decorating every surface. Abby guessed they were from well-wishers, and wished she'd thought to bring some flowers herself.

She'd stopped to admire them when Mrs Webb indicated she should go through to the room beyond.

'I'll fetch some tea in a little while,' she said. 'You go ahead now. Luke's waiting for you.'

The room that opened off the sitting area was Luke's bedroom. And it was much more austerely furnished. Although it was just as spacious in size, the quilted spread and curtains were a subtle bronze in colour, and there were few paintings on the silk-hung pale green walls.

There were no flowers here, just a huge Turkish rug that covered most of the floor, its many vivid colours adding opulence to what was otherwise a fairly spartan room.

Abby thought at first that Mrs Webb had made a mistake; that Luke wasn't in the room. Although the huge bed had evidently been slept in, there was no sign of its occupant.

And then she saw him, sitting on the window seat. She saw bare feet below loose-fitting drawstring sweat pants, a tight-fitting black tee, and one bare foot propped casually on the sill beside him.

He looked pale, and much thinner than he'd been before the accident. But he still possessed that almost indefinable magnetism that not even the puckered scar, angling down his cheek from just below his eye, could dispel.

She could see the bulge of padding from the bandages that encased his leg and upper thigh beneath the soft fabric of his sweat pants. One forearm, too, was covered with a dressing, which it hadn't been so easy to disguise.

She knew there'd been internal injuries—for one thing, his father had told her, they'd had to remove his spleen. There'd been a couple of broken ribs, one of which had punctured a lung. But, according to his surgeon, he was definitely on the mend.

There was no sign of his father now, however, but Felix, who had apparently been keeping Luke company, grinned when she came into the room.

'Yo, Abby,' he said good-humouredly, and Luke turned to give him a warning look.

'You can leave us,' Luke said as Abby hovered in the doorway. 'I'll give you a call if I need anything.'

'Yes, sir.'

Felix offered a mocking salute and, after waiting until Abby had moved further into the room, he made his exit.

The door swung closed behind him, and the sudden intimacy that created caused Abby's stomach to tighten in anticipation.

But when Luke didn't immediately say anything, she felt obliged to speak. 'Hi,' she murmured inadequately, smoothing her palms over the slight swell of her stomach. She was wearing a pleated tunic over black leggings today, but they couldn't hide her growing bulge. 'It's good to see you again.'

'Yeah.' Luke didn't sound as if he believed her. 'You'll forgive me if I don't get up?'

'Of course.' Abby caught her lower lip between her teeth. 'You must be glad to be home. How are you feeling?'

Luke's mouth tightened. 'How do I look?'

'Um—good. You look good. Better than the last time I saw you, anyway.'

'Which wouldn't be difficult,' said Luke drily. 'Tell me, how did I look when I was in a coma?

Judging by the way I look now, I wouldn't be surprised if that nausea you said you'd been suffering from returned.'

So he did remember the baby. Abby had wondered.

Her lips tightened now. 'That's not funny, Luke.'

'Did I say it was funny?' He arched a brow. 'Believe me, it's not funny at all.' He paused. 'But you didn't answer my question. Or are you too polite to say?'

'I couldn't see much of you in the hospital,' said Abby defensively. 'You were covered in bandages. How you looked was the least of my worries.'

Luke grimaced. 'Why don't I believe you?'

'I don't know.' Abby straightened her spine. 'In any case, it's the truth.'

His father had warned her to expect this. That since Luke had been allowed to come home from hospital, he'd become morose and argumentative.

Although he was supposed to be resting, he was apparently spending every morning on the computer, or haranguing his staff at Jacob's Tower. He avoided visitors. All he seemed interested in was work.

The fact that he'd had some success both on the futures market and in other, riskier, investments hadn't improved his mood. It was as if he was trying to prove to himself—and to other people—that his injuries hadn't impaired his business brain.

Or that was Oliver Morelli's interpretation, anyway.

Obviously, Luke despised his weakness. And he apparently didn't believe that his facial scars would fade. He'd told his father that he resembled a gargoyle, which Abby could see for herself was far from the truth.

She sighed, aware that he was watching her, gauging her reaction to his appearance. And, okay, he was going to have quite a scar on his cheek, but it didn't matter to her.

In his father's opinion, the damage that had been done to the muscles in his thigh was far more important. It meant there was a serious possibility that he'd never regain the strength in his legs.

Abby thought that to her he would never look any different from the man she had, possibly foolishly, fallen in love with.

But how to convince him of that?

To begin with, she'd been so optimistic. Thanks to Oliver Morelli's intervention, Abby had been allowed to spend time with Luke in the ICU.

He'd still been unconscious, and it had been a

worrying time when he'd been taken for another CT scan. His father had explained that, as well as his other injuries, they'd had to drill into his skull to relieve the pressure on his brain caused by some internal bleeding. That was no doubt why he'd slipped into a coma. But the treatment was proving a success.

Or so they'd said.

Later, with his doctor's encouragement, Abby had spent a lot of that time talking to Luke. No one had known whether he could hear her or not, but she'd taken the chance and chattered away; pretending he was asleep, instead of being deep in the coma.

But Abby couldn't help fretting the whole time she was with him. She'd half wished she'd had Harley to comfort her. It was reassuring to think that Luke, too, might have appreciated the retriever's presence. But, in the circumstances, Lori had agreed to look after him, enabling Abby to spend as much time at the hospital as she liked.

She'd continued her one-sided conversation with Luke for days, and when—miraculously— he'd eventually opened his eyes and seen her, he'd seemed glad that she was there.

He hadn't been able to say a lot. With so many bandages around his head and body, he'd seemed too confused to speak. But Abby had believed his eyes had spoken for him, and she'd driven home in her little van that evening, virtually walking on air.

Which had been a little foolish, she'd acknowledged later. Just because Luke had come round from the coma, she shouldn't run away with the idea that their relationship had radically changed. But she'd been so pleased that he was alive and lucid that she'd ignored any future consequences.

Which had been a mistake.

She definitely hadn't been prepared for the fact that the following day he'd refused to see her. And every day since, she'd had to rely on Felix or his father for updates about his health.

It was from Felix she'd learned that Luke was recovering well from the treatment. That there'd been no further complications and, pretty soon, he'd be able to go home.

'It'll be different when he's out of here,' Felix had told Abby reassuringly. 'It's this place. It makes people go crazy.'

But nothing had changed after Luke had left the hospital. And Abby couldn't understand it. After all, when she'd rushed to his bedside after hearing about the accident, he'd said he loved her. What had changed since?

Didn't he know she was the one who'd spent all her free time in the ICU? Didn't he realise

how worried she'd been about him ever since?
No matter how bad his injuries might turn out
to be, her feelings would never change.

But did Luke believe that?

It was only after Luke's father had contacted
her that she'd been told more about Luke's men-
tal condition. She and Oliver Morelli had become friends, and he'd visited the café a couple
of times to keep her up to date with developments.

His explanation was that his son didn't want
to see anyone who might remind him of the
accident. That the drugs he'd been given since
being admitted to the hospital had left him depressed and confused. He was working because
that was what he was used to doing. His personal life would have to wait.

While Abby was sure there was more to it
than that, she'd had to believe him. Until she
could speak to Luke herself, there was nothing
more she could do.

And as hard as it was to accept, there'd been
no point in forcing Luke to see her. She knew
only too well how stubborn he could be. But
surely, if she reminded him of the accident, so
must Felix, yet Felix hadn't been barred from
his room.

Now, six weeks after the accident, and three
weeks since he'd been discharged into his fa-

ther's care, she'd been granted an interview. Ironic, perhaps, but there was no other word that fitted this invitation.

And not at Oliver Morelli's house in Bath, as she'd anticipated. Apparently, Luke had insisted he recuperate in his own home in London. In consequence, his father had had to agree to a temporary change of address.

Abby couldn't help but be impressed with the house itself. A tall Georgian town house, it stretched up over four floors, with long windows flanking the main door. The door itself was painted a glossy black, and had been highly polished. There were shutters on the many windows, and a semi-circular fanlight above the door.

It was the kind of home she'd have expected a millionaire—or perhaps even a billionaire—to occupy, so what did that signify? It had certainly made her realise how remote from one another their two worlds were these days.

The man she'd met in the wine bar that night bore little resemblance to the man who was waiting to see her. She'd wondered several times why he'd insisted on rekindling their relationship. It wasn't as if he'd forgiven her for deceiving him. He still believed that Harry had been the innocent party all along.

Inside, the house was equally impressive. A

long hall led to the back of the house, where a conservatory reflected the warmth of the morning sun. A semi-circular table against the wall in the hall boasted a bowl of autumn flowers, with several greetings cards, evidently from well-wishers, lying on a silver tray.

Abby had only glimpsed the rooms below as she'd mounted the curving staircase with the housekeeper. But, again, her impression had been of understated elegance, much different from the steel and chrome apartment she had once shared with Harry Laurence all those years ago.

Despite the invitation, Abby was no longer optimistic about this visit. She was sure Oliver Morelli had persuaded Luke to see her, and that was the last thing she wanted in the present circumstances. She was supremely conscious of her pregnancy. And of the fact that aside from Lori—and Luke, of course—she'd told no one about the baby.

Luke had apparently not told anyone either. And although she'd been tempted to tell his father, and Felix, she was loath to do anything that might alienate her even more from Luke.

As she stood there now, she was intensely conscious of her own appearance. Already her clothes were getting tighter, and her breasts were spilling out of her skimpy bra.

She was no longer the slender woman Luke had encountered when he'd come into the café that first morning almost four months ago. And of the two of them, she was very much afraid she had changed the most.

She half wished she hadn't come.

Now Luke indicated an armchair at right angles to the window seat. 'Sit down,' he said, lifting his foot from the sill and placing it on the floor.

She noticed the care with which he moved, but he couldn't quite hide the twinge of pain that crossed his face as he did so. However, he quickly disguised it, reaching for a crutch that was lying beside him and pulling himself to his feet.

Abby, who had taken him at his word and seated herself in the armchair, now looked up at him in some confusion. 'Where are you going? Is something wrong?'

'Wrong?' Luke's tone was sardonic. 'What could be wrong?' He paused and took a careful step away from the window. 'I just want to give you something, that's all.'

'To give me something?' Abby repeated blankly, not entirely liking the sound of that.

'Relax,' he said, heading for a chest of drawers at the far side of the room. 'This might be the last time we see one another for some time, so I want to make sure you have everything you need.'

Abby's mouth dropped open. 'I beg your pardon?' she said, hardly daring to believe what she'd heard.

'This may be the last time—' he began again, but she interrupted him.

'Yes, I know what you said,' she exclaimed, halting him in his tracks. 'I just don't—' She broke off and then started again, more calmly. 'What are you talking about?'

Luke's dark eyes narrowed. 'I should have thought that was perfectly obvious,' he said. 'I don't think we should see one another again.'

'Why? That's not what you said the last time you came to the café.'

He took a steadying breath and continued on towards the cabinet. 'Give me a moment. Then you'll understand.'

'I doubt it.' Abby got to her feet. 'Are you supposed to be walking around like this?' she asked tersely. 'You're very—'

'Weak?' he broke in mockingly. 'Yes, I can see how shocked you were by my appearance. I'm no longer the attractive catch you thought I was.'

'Don't be so ridiculous!' Abby stared at him incredulously. 'I was about to say, you're very pale.' She paused and then went on shortly, 'I didn't realise you were so vain, Luke.'

Luke had his back to her, but she saw him hunch his shoulders. 'I'm not vain, Abby. Just realistic.'

'Really?' Abby could feel her own temper rising. 'So do I take it that the only reason you've refused to see me all these weeks is because you were afraid I might not like your appearance?'

'Um—no,' he said honestly, still not looking at her. 'I don't really think you're that shallow.'

'Well, thanks. I think.'

'But it isn't fair to expect you to tie yourself to a man who's both physically and mentally flawed,' he continued harshly. 'You've had a bad experience once. I doubt if you want to suffer another.'

CHAPTER SIXTEEN

LUKE KNEW THAT Abby was on her feet now. She expelled what sounded like an impatient breath, and he guessed she was wondering what the hell he meant.

But now, after what Felix had found out, Luke knew for sure that Harry Laurence had been as much of a bastard as he'd suspected, he couldn't inflict his own problems on her, as well.

She was too loyal; she had too much integrity. As witnessed by the way she'd stayed with her ex-husband, long after she'd learned what manner of man he was.

However foolish Luke still considered that had been.

'I don't understand,' she said brusquely. 'Are you talking about Harry?'

'Who else?'

Abby sucked in a breath. 'But you know nothing about Harry,' she said impatiently. 'And I can tell you this, you're nothing like him.'

'You think?'

Luke had reached the bureau now, and he attempted to pull open the bottom drawer. But it was difficult to bend and open a two-handled drawer with only one hand. He swore his frustration as the crutch slipped away.

And knew he would have fallen if Abby hadn't immediately seen his difficulties and rushed to help him. Her slim arms encircled his waist, and he felt the slight swell of her body close against the curve of his spine.

It was the baby, he thought, his jaw tightening with the knowledge of what he was about to deny himself. The urge to turn and hold her close against his taut body was almost irresistible, but he no longer had the right to do so.

'You could have asked me to get whatever it is for you,' Abby exclaimed somewhat breathlessly as he attempted to regain his balance. 'Surely it can't be so important that you're willing to risk your health.'

'I'm not risking my health.' Luke was unable to hide his bitterness. 'It was just a bit of poor judgement, that's all. Something I'm quite familiar with, believe me.'

'If you're implying it was your poor judgement that caused the accident, you couldn't be more wrong,' protested Abby, her warm breath fanning the back of his neck. 'Look, why don't you sit down and let me get whatever you need?'

Luke allowed himself to rest against her for a few moments longer, revelling in the heat of her nearness, inhaling the fragrant scent of her skin.

But his response quickly became far too sexual, and he couldn't afford to indulge in that kind of madness again. Not if he wanted to give her the chance to start a new life without any restrictions at all.

Nevertheless, Abby didn't seem in any hurry to let him go. Indeed, her hands spread caressingly against his stomach and he knew that, any second, she was going to discover he wasn't as controlled as he'd like to pretend.

However, when he would have drawn away, she rested her forehead against his back, and whispered softly, 'Can't we talk about this? You can't possibly imagine I want our relationship to end, just because you don't think you're the handsome stud you used to be.'

Luke groaned. 'I was never a handsome stud,' he muttered cynically. 'But I won't be a burden on you, Abby. I know now how you must have suffered with Laurence, and you deserve a better chance at life.'

Abby went still, and, after making sure he was unlikely to fall, she moved round him so she could see his face. 'You know now?' she echoed. 'How do you know? About Harry, I mean?' She looked doubtful for a moment.

Luke leaned heavily on his crutch. This was the difficult part and he knew it.

'Harry's in prison,' he told her unwillingly. 'Did you know?'

'In prison?' Abby stared at him incredulously. 'No. I didn't know that. How could I?'

She paused, evidently digesting what he'd said. Then, 'But how do you know?' she asked, before a look of dismay crossed her face as the answer came to her. 'You've had him investigated, haven't you? You didn't take my word, so you decided to check my story out for yourself.'

Luke blew out a breath. 'That's not entirely true.' He'd known this might happen; that was one of the reasons why he'd put off seeing her for so long.

'Before the accident,' he went on. 'Before I realised that I—' He almost said *that I loved you*, but he managed to bite the words back. 'Well, just accept that it was before the accident, I asked Felix to find out what Laurence was doing these days. I had no idea that the accident would prevent me from telling you what I'd done.'

Abby stepped back from him. 'You asked Felix?' She shook her head. 'No. He would have told me.'

'Felix wouldn't tell you anything without my permission,' said Luke, expelling a weary breath. 'He knew you'd think I'd been checking up on you.'

'You had.'

'Not in the way you mean,' declared Luke roughly. 'If you must know, I'd already decided that there had to be more to your relationship with Laurence than I'd originally thought,' he said tiredly, wishing he could sit down. 'I actually wanted to kill him. Which would have given me a great deal of pleasure, but I didn't get the chance.'

'And you just accidentally discovered that Harry was in prison,' she said sceptically. 'How convenient was that.'

'It wasn't convenient at all actually.' Luke sighed. 'Felix came to see me while I was in the hospital. I'd been depressed for days, and he foolishly thought that knowing your ex-husband was in prison might give me some encouragement to get well.'

Abby frowned. 'And he thought this, why?'

'Don't be naïve.' Luke exhaled noisily. 'Felix isn't a fool. He knew—*knows*—how I feel about you.'

Abby hesitated, and he could tell his words had registered with her, however reckless they had been. 'Well, I still don't understand. How did he find out about Harry?'

Luke swayed a little, but he managed to stay

on his feet as he said, 'Felix knew someone who worked in the City, and, when he mentioned Laurence's name, this guy said Harry had been convicted of abusing his wife.'

'Abusing his wife?' Abby was taken aback. 'But I've never—'

'I got that.' Luke was bitter now. 'I couldn't understand why.'

He shook his head. That wasn't something he wanted to get into right now. 'But apparently, he'd married again a couple of years ago.'

'And when were you going to tell me this?'

'I wasn't,' he said. 'I knew what you'd think. But circumstances alter cases.'

Luke blew out a breath, abandoning any hope of opening the chest of drawers for the present. He dragged himself to the bed and lowered himself onto the mattress.

'I'm sorry,' he said heavily. 'You'll have to give me a minute. I guess my legs are not as strong as I thought.'

Immediately, Abby's expression changed, her indignation giving way to anxiety. Abandoning her position, she came to join him on the bed, sitting down beside him and gazing at him with unconcealed concern.

'I'm the one who should be sorry,' she murmured, hesitating only a moment before rubbing his back with a gentle hand. 'I should have realised you're still recovering from surgery. We can continue this conversation when you're feeling better—'

'No!'

Luke knew he had to get this over with now, before he gave into the desire to be with her. The feel of her hand massaging his back was far too appealing. But he must remember why he'd brought her here.

Yet he could feel the heat of her hand through his tee shirt, feel her thigh warm against his hip. His skin prickled with the knowledge that this might be the last time they'd be alone together like this. But whatever happened, he had to keep his head.

Yet it was well-nigh impossible.

'Abby,' he said hoarsely, desperate to say what needed to be said before he lost the will to do so.

However, although she might feel like punishing him for his arrogance, Abby's hand moved up to his shoulder, and from there to the nape of his neck.

The feel of her cool fingers against his skin was a torment. He could feel his pulse pounding, the blood searing hotly through his veins. He felt a constriction in his chest that expanded as he gazed at her; at the delicate curve of her cheekbones, at the soft vulnerability of her mouth.

'I would never hurt you,' he grated. It was not what he'd planned to say and his hands balled into fists on his thighs. 'You've got to believe that.'

'I do believe it.' Her fingers brushed the growth of stubble on his jawline. 'But you didn't trust me. You never did.'

Luke forced himself to flinch away from that caressing touch. He was half afraid that if she touched his scars, he'd never find the strength to let her go.

His breath hitched, and then, although it was much too late to do so, he tried to explain.

'I would have told you about Harry,' he said unsteadily. 'But I suppose what bugged me was the fact that you'd stayed with a man like him, even knowing how he was treating you. Why in God's name didn't you leave him?'

Abby sighed. 'I had my reasons—'

Luke stiffened. 'You loved him?'

'I don't think I ever loved him,' she admitted ruefully. 'But my mother liked him and I suppose I trusted her judgement.'

'And later?'

Abby's fingers curled over his scalp, finding the roughened patch of shaved skin where they'd drilled into his skull. Her breathing quickened, as if at the renewed realisation that he could have died, and Luke felt his nerves tighten in response.

She swallowed convulsively, but, like him, she obviously felt compelled to go on.

'I suppose my mother thought he would look after me. He had a good job, a nice apartment. She knew nothing about the way he treated me. Harry was careful not to do anything that might arouse her suspicions.'

Luke captured her tormenting fingers in his and brought her hand down to rest on his knees. 'And when he started abusing you?' he asked huskily.

'Oh...' Abby's voice broke, and when she continued, her tone was much lower. 'So you believe me?'

'I'd suspected it for some time,' said Luke, massaging her knuckles with unsteady fingers. 'Even that night in the wine bar, I noticed you had bruises on your neck. What I still don't understand is why you didn't leave him.'

'But you never asked why, did you?' she murmured unevenly.

'Perhaps I didn't want to know the answer,' said Luke honestly. He groaned. 'Every time I thought of you two together... God!'

'My mother became terminally ill about two years after Harry and I got married,' Abby broke in quickly. 'I had already realised that the marriage wasn't going to work, but…'

She broke off and pressed her lips together before going on, 'But my mother needed constant nursing care, and my salary wasn't going to pay for that or for a decent nursing home when she needed one. Harry told my mother that she didn't have to worry. He'd take care of all of it.'

'So he paid?'

Abby nodded.

Luke stared at her. 'Why didn't you tell me?'

'When?' Abby withdrew her hand from his, twisting her fingers together in her lap. 'That first day you came to the café, when you accused me of cheating on my husband? Or later, when, although you were making love to me, you were making it plain that you'd never trust a woman like me?'

Luke scowled. 'What about the night you arranged to meet me at the wine bar? Couldn't you have told me then?'

'Oh, right.' Abby gave a little cry and pushed herself up from the bed, raking trembling hands through her hair. 'How would I have phrased that, I wonder?'

She glanced back at him over her shoulder, her expression pained.

'Let me see, how about—*by the way, Luke, I*

should have told you, I'm married. My husband is abusing me, but he's only agreed to go on paying for my mother's palliative care if I don't tell anyone about it.' Her lips twisted. 'Yeah, I can quite see how that would have worked.'

Luke couldn't listen to any more. He caught her wrist and pulled her down onto the bed again. Then, before he could stop himself, he hooked his hand behind her head and brought her mouth to his.

'I'm sorry,' he said against her lips. 'I'm sorry. I've been such a fool. Will you ever forgive me?'

He heard her catch her breath, but she didn't draw back. And what began as an attempt to make amends for his past sins quickly became a hungry assault on his senses. It might have been weeks since he'd held her in his arms, but she felt so right there, and he didn't want to let her go.

Ignoring the pain in his arm, he bore her back against the tumbled sheets and covered her with his body. The soft sweat pants he was wearing did nothing to disguise the erection pushing against the cotton, an erection that fitted so perfectly into the yielding juncture of her thighs.

One of her hands slid down between them, finding the throbbing pulse of his arousal before slipping inside his pants.

Her fingers closed around him and Luke's senses spun.

He wanted her. Dear God, he wanted to be with her. Not just for now, but always. Did he have the right to feel this way? When he might be an invalid for the rest of his life?

No!

He was soon aware that he was in danger of losing what little self-respect he had left. When he pulled away, she was forced to release him, and for a moment he could only lie on his back beside her, striving for control.

When his breathing eventually steadied, he pushed himself up into a sitting position again. And from there, he used the crutch to haul himself to his feet and slowly make his way back to the chest of drawers.

This time he managed to get the drawer open, and he pulled out the sheaf of documents safe inside a green plastic file.

Then he turned and made his way back; but not to the bed. To his earlier position on the window seat.

CHAPTER SEVENTEEN

'LUKE?' ABBY FROWNED, propping herself up on her elbows. 'Why are you sitting over there?'

Luke pulled a wry face. 'Because I don't trust myself to sit beside you. Abby, much as I want to be with you, it's not going to happen.'

Abby sat up then and stared at him. 'What's not going to happen?'

'You. Me. Us.' He avoided her eyes by bending over the file he'd collected from the drawer. 'You must have wondered why I asked you to come and see me today.'

Abby frowned. 'I was beginning to think it was because you'd come to your senses.'

'Well, yes.' Luke's mouth twisted, and he cast her a rueful glance. 'In a manner of speaking, you could be right.' He paused. 'Though not in the way you perhaps mean.'

Abby was tense now. 'Go on,' she said, half knowing she wasn't going to like what he had to say.

Meanwhile, Luke had drawn out a sheaf of official-looking documents, and, putting the plastic folder aside, he lifted his head and looked at her.

'I suppose I should have had my solicitor do this,' he said, 'but I gave in to my desire to see you again and decided to speak to you myself.'

'Speak to me about what?' Abby was confused. 'If this has something to with the accident—'

'It has,' he broke in before she could continue. 'Apart from my obvious injuries, there are complications. I'm informed that, at the least, there's no guarantee that I'll ever regain the full use of my legs.'

'So?' Abby was confused. 'You know I'll be there for you, whatever happens.'

'No.' Luke's tone was harsh. 'Do you think I want you to spend the rest of your life looking after an invalid? I could spend half my life in a wheelchair. I don't want that for you.'

Abby took a disbelieving breath. 'And what about what I want?'

'Abby, I know you mean well, but this isn't something to be taken lightly. I haven't even spoken to you about the other injuries I've had.'

'I know they had to relieve the pressure on your brain by drilling a hole in your skull,' said

Abby defensively. 'Your father said that had been a complete success.'

'How would he know?' Luke was impatient. 'There are always doubts about how successful that kind of treatment has been.'

'But your brain is working perfectly well,' she insisted vehemently. 'You know that.'

'And what if I had a relapse? What if I became paralysed or worse?'

'We'd face that if it happened.' Abby sighed. 'Don't be pessimistic, Luke. No one knows what's round the corner. Even me.'

'Which is very brave of you, but you have to be practical.' For a moment, his eyes dropped to the slight swell of her stomach and his lips compressed. 'You're going to have enough to cope with, what with the baby. I would only create more problems for you.'

Abby's lips tightened. 'You don't think it's more important for the baby—our baby—to know its father?' she demanded. 'Luke, the baby needs you. I need you. I love you. Isn't that enough?'

Luke bent his head over the papers he was holding, and, instead of answering her, said, 'I've made arrangements for you, and the baby. And I'll get to them in a moment.'

'Luke…'

'But first, I want to tell you that the development will go ahead as planned. However, I've made certain amendments to my original drawings, which I think you'll approve of.'

'Luke, you shouldn't be thinking about such things right now.'

'There will still be a supermarket,' he persisted doggedly. 'But I've decided to make a small mall of individual shops leading to the bigger premises.'

He paused and then continued, 'Naturally, you and the other tenants will have the option of renting one of these units; and I'm assured that this will give you all the opportunity to gain from passing trade.'

He lifted an architectural drawing from the file and unfolded it on the window seat beside him. 'This is a copy of the plans being presented to the committee and, naturally, you'll all be able to view them before any decision is made.'

Abby shook her head. 'You didn't have to do this,' she protested.

'Oh, I did,' he said firmly. 'I'd decided on the changes before—well, before the crash. I'm also arranging for the rents to be capped. Which should please your friend, Hughes.'

'He's not my friend,' said Abby flatly. 'But you're right. He'll think he's won.'

Luke looked at her now. 'Do you think I care what he thinks?' he demanded. 'I'm not doing this for him. I'm doing it for you. I don't want to deprive you of your livelihood, just in case you refuse my help.'

'What help?'

'I'm coming to that.' Luke took a steadying breath. 'If you'll just give me a moment…'

Instead of doing that, Abby got to her feet and came across to the window seat to sit next to him. Luke moved aside so his hip was not touching hers, and she persuaded herself it was because his thigh still pained him. A lot.

Picking up the plans to move them aside, she saw at once what Luke was describing to her. It was a perfect blend of ancient and modern; a sleek supermarket, approached by a neat row of small, more traditional units.

'This is what you've been doing?' she asked, forcing him to meet her eyes.

'Well, my architect,' he agreed modestly. 'But you can tell Hughes that the shops he so badly wanted to preserve didn't fall into the necessary category for conservation.'

Abby pulled a face. 'I never thought they did.' She folded the plans again and put them aside. 'Thank you,' she said. 'There are going to be some very relieved shopkeepers.'

'Good.'

'Okay.' Abby blew out a breath. 'So let's talk

about us. Because there is an "us", whatever you say.'

'I'm coming to that.'

'Not quickly enough,' said Abby, gazing at him with accusing eyes. 'I hope you're not about to try and buy me off.'

Luke sucked in a breath. 'I wouldn't put it quite like that,' he said. 'But I do want to do what's best for you and the baby—'

'So do I.'

'—and by ensuring you are financially secure, I won't feel so bad about you having to cope alone.'

Abby's brows drew together. 'What do you mean, having to cope alone?'

Luke rolled his lips inward. Then he said quietly, 'I'm thinking of spending some time abroad.'

'Abroad?' Abby's stomach dropped. 'Where abroad?'

'I haven't decided yet. As you can see, I'm not really fit to travel at present.'

'And you plan to go alone?'

'Of course, alone.' Luke ran an impatient hand over his scalp. His hair was growing back over the spot they'd shaved, and a dark strand fell appealingly over his forehead. 'Apart from Felix, that is. I don't imagine he'll let me go far without him.'

Abby could hardly bear to look at him. 'But I don't have that right. Is that what you're saying?' she demanded painfully. 'For God's sake, Luke, you said you loved me. I'm having your child. Doesn't that mean anything to you?'

'Of course, it means something,' he retorted, his frustration giving way to anger. 'Do you think this is what I want to say, Abby? Do you think I want to go and live in some Godforsaken country where I'll know nobody?'

With a strength she guessed was born of a sense of inadequacy, he managed to get to his feet. 'But I can't stay here, not when being near you is such a temptation. I was planning to ask you to marry me. But that would be pure indulgence now.'

'Then don't indulge yourself, indulge me,' exclaimed Abby emotionally. Getting to her feet, she successfully blocked him when he would have moved away. 'Indulge your baby,' she added huskily, drawing the hand that wasn't clutching his crutch to her stomach. 'I need you. We both need you. Are you honestly prepared to deny you need us, too?'

Luke stared down at her with tortured eyes. 'You know the answer to that as well as me.'

'So why hesitate?' Abby moved closer and slipped her arms about him, ignoring his instinctive attempt to move away.

'Can't you see, we can face whatever problems there are together? Nothing is easy, Luke. But so long as we love one another, nothing can keep us apart.'

'But you don't deserve this!'

'*You* don't deserve this,' countered Abby huskily.

'But after the life you had with Laurence,' Luke protested, 'I won't be a burden to you.'

'You couldn't be a burden to me if you tried,' she whispered, reaching up to bestow a warm kiss at the corner of his mouth. 'I want to live with you. I want to share my life with you.' She pulled a face. 'I don't honestly care if you marry me or not, so long as you don't send me away.'

Luke's jaw tensed. 'It's what I should do,' he said, but he didn't sound as certain as he'd done before.

'What you should do is make love to me,' said Abby huskily. 'Then tell me there's no future for us together.'

Some time later, someone knocked at the bedroom door.

Luke, who had been sound asleep moments before, stirred reluctantly. Feeling the warmth of a bare thigh cradled against the bandage that encircled his leg, Luke turned his head to find Abby was stirring, too.

With her hair spread silkily across his pillow and her breasts crushed softly against his uninjured arm, she looked incredibly sexy and incredibly beautiful. And he was loath to speak and break the spell that had held them in its magical grip for the past—he glanced at his watch—almost an hour.

But Abby was awake, and her smile was so joyous that Luke couldn't prevent the urge to say roughly, 'God, I love you. How in hell am I going to let you go?'

'You're not,' declared Abby confidently, gathering the sheets about her and leaning over to kiss his injured cheek.

Then her brows arched mischievously. 'But now I'd better see who that is before they think I've kidnapped you.'

Luke shook his head. 'Like that's going to happen,' he muttered and she gurgled with laughter.

'It could,' she assured him, reaching for her tunic and pulling it over her head. 'In any case, I think it's your housekeeper. She said she was going to bring some tea.'

'Tea!' Luke grimaced. 'I'll need something stronger than tea if I'm going to ask you to marry me.'

Abby, who had evidently decided not to bother with her leggings, had been heading for the door when he spoke. But now, she turned, her mouth parting in stunned disbelief.

'You can't say something like that and not expect me to respond,' she whispered, staring at him, and Luke pushed himself up on his elbows and regarded her inquiringly.

'Well?' he countered. 'What are you going to do about it?'

Another knock sounded at the door, and Abby hesitated, torn between the need to open it and the equally—if not more—urgent need to return to the bed.

'Damn you, Luke,' she said helplessly, and, ignoring the other summons, she returned to the bed.

'Is that any way to answer a proposal?' he mocked teasingly, and Abby took his face between her hands and bestowed a hungry kiss on his mouth.

'No,' she agreed. 'But my answer's the same, anyway. It's yes, you wicked man.'

She trembled when he pulled her down onto the bed beside him and returned her kiss with interest. He covered her with his body, his tongue slipping possessively into her mouth so that she moaned with pleasure.

And whoever had been at the door evidently decided that tea wasn't needed at the moment.

EPILOGUE

It WAS LATE afternoon when Luke turned into the gates of the cottage that he and Abby had bought just under a year ago.

As the SUV negotiated the leaf-strewn curve of the drive and the wisteria-hung walls of the house came into view, Abby thought again how lucky they were having a place like this to escape to.

Initially, when Luke had suggested buying a cottage near his father's home in Bath, Abby had had visions of a Cotswold cottage, with maybe a thatched roof or a shingled portico.

But she should have known better. This cottage more properly resembled a small country house, with half a dozen bedrooms and bathrooms and a live-in housekeeper, who looked after the place all year round.

Even so, Mrs Bainbridge, whose husband took care of the grounds of the property, was a tactful, sensitive soul, who gave them all the space they needed. Indeed, there were evenings when she retired to the annexe she shared with her husband, and left Abby in charge of the kitchen.

Which suited Abby's lingering catering tendencies very well.

Now Luke brought the car to a halt on the gravelled forecourt and Abby cast a glance over her shoulder. Their eighteen-month-old son, Matthew Oliver Morelli, was drowsing in his booster seat, with Harley strapped in a seat beside him.

Matthew had been awake for most of the journey from London, chattering away in his own inimitable style. He'd only fallen asleep when the roads grew narrower and there were tall hedgerows on either side of the car blocking his view. Abby guessed Harley was glad of the reprieve. Matthew could be very noisy at times.

'Do you think he'll let us get the car unpacked before he decides he wants to join in?' asked Luke drily, giving his wife a rueful grin.

'Oh, I'm sure Harley will let you do that,' she answered mischievously. 'So long as Mrs Bainbridge has got something tasty for his supper.'

Luke grimaced, and, reaching over, turned his wife's face towards him for an intimate kiss. 'I want something tasty before my supper,' he remarked, allowing his tongue to brush her lips as he withdrew. 'Do you think you can accommodate me?'

Abby's breathing quickened. Nothing had changed. Luke had only to touch her and she wanted to wind herself about him. After almost two years of marriage, she still melted every time he kissed her.

'If your son settles down after his bath, I may be able to help you,' she said coyly, tugging on a strand of the dark blonde hair that hung loosely about her shoulders. 'But I'm making no promises.'

Luke shook his head, permitting himself another disturbing caress before thrusting open the car door. 'You are a terrible tease, Mrs Morelli,' he said thickly. 'And here's Mrs Bainbridge, right on cue.'

The housekeeper, an attractive older woman in her sixties, had opened the door and stood beaming on the threshold.

She always seemed pleased to see them, and their baby son had definitely captured both her and her husband's hearts.

'Did you have a good journey?' asked Mrs Bainbridge as she hefted the bag containing the baby's things from the boot.

Abby slid out to join her, opening the rear door and releasing Harley from his harness. 'Not bad,' she said. 'The traffic wasn't too horrendous. Now, behave yourself, Harls,' she called warningly as the retriever bounded towards Mr Bainbridge, who was culling the box hedges that edged the stretch of lawn at the front of the house. She exchanged a smile with the groundsman. 'How are you, Mr B? Still working hard, I see.'

'Getting there, Mrs Morelli, getting there,' he said, bending down to tug Harley's ears, and his wife gave him a conservative look.

'He's just been in for a cup of tea and a hot scone,' she remarked drily. 'He's not overworked, Mrs Morelli. Not now you've employed that boy, Sam, to help him out.'

Luke, who had taken a little longer to get out of the vehicle, now straightened his spine with some relief. Although it was over two years since the accident, he still suffered some stiffness in his right thigh, particularly if he'd been in one position for too long.

But he'd made miraculous progress, due in no small part to the fact that he was happier now than he'd ever been in his life. Oliver Morelli considered Abby the prime reason for his son's recovery, and he'd become very fond of his daughter-in-law. Which was why, whenever they were staying at the cottage, he was a frequent visitor.

'It's been a lovely day today, and they say

it's going to be a fine weekend,' remarked Mrs Bainbridge, glancing into the back of the car. 'Would you like me to get the baby out of his chair?'

'I'll do it,' said Luke at once, exchanging a speaking look with Abby. They both knew Mrs Bainbridge was always eager to get her hands on their young son.

'It should be a good weekend,' said Abby, gathering a couple of bags and following the older woman into the house. 'It's good to be here. It was raining in London.'

'Awful place,' exclaimed Mrs Bainbridge, leading the way along the carpeted hall to the stairs. 'I'm always saying to Joe that you and Mr Morelli—and the little one, of course—should move down here permanently. Now that Mr Morelli does a lot of his work online, there's no need for him to go into the office every day.'

Abby hid a smile. Luke didn't go into the office every day, even when they were in London. Indeed, since their marriage, he'd delegated a lot of his work to his vice presidents. The various departments functioned satisfactorily for the most part, enabling him to spend more time with his wife and family.

They'd married as soon as Luke was capable of standing without support, which had been about three months after the accident. Initially, he'd had to attend hospital on a regular basis, for follow-up examinations and physiotherapy.

He'd decided not to have plastic surgery on his face, after Abby had said she rather liked his scar. She'd said it made him look like a pirate, and she'd always loved pirates when she was a girl.

They'd spent Christmas and New Year with Luke's father, before returning to London so that Abby could have the baby at the hospital in Paddington, where she'd been looked after during her pregnancy.

Then a month after Matthew's birth, she and Luke had taken three weeks away in lieu of a honeymoon.

Oliver Morelli had insisted they both needed a break, and he'd been responsible for contacting one of the foremost agencies in London and hiring a nanny to look after the baby.

Matthew and the nanny had stayed with Luke's father while they were away, and since then the nanny had become a permanent fixture in the London house.

However, she didn't usually accompany them to the cottage, as Mrs Bainbridge would have been most put out if she hadn't been called upon to babysit, when necessary.

The 'honeymoon' had been magical. They'd

spent most of the time in Hawaii, where Luke had been able to have a complete rest.

The weather had been wonderful, and they'd slept and made love, swum and made love, and made love just for the hell of it. It had actually been hard to leave paradise behind and return to earth.

It had been good to see their baby son again, and Felix, of course.

Abby had come to depend on Felix while Luke was still having treatment. He'd taken over the care of Harley when she moved to London, and he'd been responsible for the retriever not missing his country walks. Abby hadn't realised how many parks there were until Felix took control.

Now, after Mrs Bainbridge had deposited Matthew's bag and departed, Abby looked round the bedroom she shared with Luke with real pleasure.

Probably because they had chosen this house together, Abby felt a real connection to the rooms and everything in them. When he'd been well enough to walk, she and Luke had spent days touring auction rooms and antique shops, looking for the right kind of furniture. They'd wanted period pieces to fit their new home.

In consequence, although it wasn't as elegant as the Eaton Close house, the cottage was filled with tables and cabinets that in turn were filled with all the souvenirs they'd picked up on their travels.

The development in Ashford-St-James, which had initially brought them back together, was going ahead as planned. The small shops and Abby's café were still operating. She had been lucky enough to find someone to run the café for her, and, as the young woman was Lori's sister, there'd been no friction between them.

The supermarket being erected behind was almost finished. When it was, the row of shops would then be demolished, before being resurrected when the new mall was complete.

The whole development had been designed to cause the least amount of upset. Even Greg Hughes had had to admit that Luke was a pretty decent guy.

Decent wasn't the word for him, thought Abby dreamily. He was the man she had always wanted to marry, the only man that she had ever loved.

Speaking of which, she smiled as Luke came into the bedroom carrying their son. Matthew was awake and chattering away to his father. She and Luke could only understand a word or two as yet, but Matthew was quickly learning how to get his own way.

'I need a shower,' said Luke, setting Matthew

down so that he could toddle across the floor to his mother. His lips twitched. 'Want to join me?'

'I might,' said Abby consideringly. 'But your son needs his bath and his supper first.'

'Can't Mrs B do that?' asked Luke persuasively, coming to drop a lazy kiss on her cheek. 'You know how she loves to be put in charge.'

Abby smiled. 'She's not the only one,' she remarked drily, stopping the little boy when he tried to pull away. 'You'll just have to go and talk to Joe until I'm finished.'

Luke gave a resigned sigh. 'I sometimes think we should bring Mrs Darnley down here with us,' he said, naming the nanny who worked for them in London, and Abby gave him a reproving look.

'Wasn't it your idea that coming here meant we three could be alone together?' she reminded him, picking up Matthew and loving the way he nestled his head into the curve of her neck. Then, carrying him through to the adjoining nursery, she added, 'Of course, if you've decided you'd like her to join us for all her meals, because there is no separate apartment for her here, then I can get on the phone right—'

But what she was going to say was stifled by her husband, wrapping his arm about both of them and burying his face in her shoulder.

'You dare,' he muttered threateningly, and Matthew lifted a pink-knuckled hand to push him away.

'No, Daddy,' he said, two words that were part of his limited vocabulary, and Abby giggled uncontrollably.

'There,' she said. 'You have your answer. Now, go and annoy someone else until Matthew has had his bath.'

The shower was running when Abby opened the bathroom door. Matthew was now sound asleep in his cot in the nursery, and, after shedding all but her bra and panties, Abby tiptoed to the shower door and peeped inside.

Luke saw her at once. 'Come in,' he said huskily. 'I've been waiting for you.'

'I'll just finish undressing,' she began, but Luke put out his hand and pulled her into the steamy cubicle with him.

'Let me,' he told her thickly. Pulling her back against him, he loosened the front fastening of her bra. The bra slipped to the floor and he let his hands slide down over her breasts until they reached the waistband of her lacy briefs. 'Mmm, you're ready for me,' he said, cupping the place between her legs. 'Your panties are wet.'

'I think that's the shower,' Abby protested breathlessly, but Luke shook his head.

His finger probed beneath the lace and found her throbbing core. 'The water from the shower can't reach where I'm reaching,' he said, allowing two fingers to slide inside her.

'You're hot and wet. And don't I love it?'

He continued to press her back against him for a moment, but when his own body started to protest, he quickly disposed of her panties.

'God, I want you,' he muttered, swinging her round to face him, before easing her back against the glass wall. He was fully aroused, she saw, allowing her hands to drift down over his chest to his stomach. Then, even lower, until he gave a muffled groan.

'Wait,' he groaned and reached for the shower gel. As he was pouring some into his palm, Abby filched a little and eased her hand down between his legs.

'Abby,' he said hoarsely as she smoothed some over his bulging manhood. 'Do you know what you're doing to me? Have a bit of compassion.'

Abby only gurgled with laughter and, despite the lingering weakness in his thigh, Luke didn't hesitate any longer. He lifted her against the glass wall and thrust into her, embedding himself deeply in her velvety sheath.

Abby wrapped her legs around his hips as he filled her completely. She was already aroused and she felt her body tighten and expand as he pressed even deeper into her core.

She was almost sorry when she felt her body beginning to shudder and felt his answering response in his tightening grasp.

She'd wanted to prolong the excitement, but, with one final penetration, he had them both giving in to a shattering release.

Even when Luke lowered her feet to the floor of the cubicle, Abby was still quivering. But Luke wasn't finished, and he soaped his hands and massaged her breasts and the cleft between her buttocks until she was trembling with expectancy again.

This time, after rinsing off the soap, Luke picked her up and carried her into their bedroom. Uncaring that their bodies were still wet, he made love to her again, with all the power and urgency of their first encounter.

Afterwards, as Abby lay drowsing, her body pleasantly exhausted from Luke's demands, he said softly, 'I love you, Mrs Morelli. I want you to know my love for you grows stronger every day we're together.'

Abby reached up and wound her arms around his neck. She bestowed a warm kiss to the corner of his mouth. 'I love you, too, Mr Morelli,' she murmured. She drew back to look into his eyes. 'I suspect I've loved you since that evening I met you in the wine bar.'

'Then it's just as well I found you when I did,' he responded, burying his face in the hollow between her breasts. 'I'd hate to think you might have married someone else.'

'Not a chance,' said Abby emotively, and Luke gave a contented sigh.

'You know, I was a fool to think you could be my mistress,' he murmured. 'I think you were always meant to be my wife.'

* * * * *

If you enjoyed this story, check out these other great reads from Anne Mather

A FORBIDDEN TEMPTATION
INNOCENT VIRGIN, WILD SURRENDER
HIS FORBIDDEN PASSION
THE BRAZILIAN MILLIONAIRE'S
LOVE-CHILD
MENDEZ'S MISTRESS

Available now!

LARGER-PRINT BOOKS!
GET 2 FREE LARGER-PRINT NOVELS PLUS
2 FREE GIFTS!

◊ HARLEQUIN®

Romance

From the Heart, For the Heart

YES! Please send me 2 FREE LARGER-PRINT Harlequin® Romance novels and my 2 FREE gifts (gifts are worth about $10). After receiving them, if I don't wish to receive any more books, I can return the shipping statement marked "cancel." If I don't cancel, I will receive 4 brand-new novels every month and be billed just $5.09 per book in the U.S. or $5.49 per book in Canada. That's a savings of at least 15% off the cover price! It's quite a bargain! Shipping and handling is just 50¢ per book in the U.S. and 75¢ per book in Canada.* I understand that accepting the 2 free books and gifts places me under no obligation to buy anything. I can always return a shipment and cancel at any time. Even if I never buy another book, the two free books and gifts are mine to keep forever.

119/319 HDN GHWC

Name	(PLEASE PRINT)

Address		Apt. #

City	State/Prov.	Zip/Postal Code

Signature (if under 18, a parent or guardian must sign)

Mail to the Reader Service:
IN U.S.A.: P.O. Box 1867, Buffalo, NY 14240-1867
IN CANADA: P.O. Box 609, Fort Erie, Ontario L2A 5X3
Want to try two free books from another line?
Call 1-800-873-8635 or visit www.ReaderService.com.

* Terms and prices subject to change without notice. Prices do not include applicable taxes. Sales tax applicable in N.Y. Canadian residents will be charged applicable taxes. Offer not valid in Quebec. This offer is limited to one order per household. Not valid for current subscribers to Harlequin Romance Larger-Print books. All orders subject to credit approval. Credit or debit balances in a customer's account(s) may be offset by any other outstanding balance owed by or to the customer. Please allow 4 to 6 weeks for delivery. Offer available while quantities last.

Your Privacy—The Reader Service is committed to protecting your privacy. Our Privacy Policy is available online at www.ReaderService.com or upon request from the Reader Service.

We make a portion of our mailing list available to reputable third parties that offer products we believe may interest you. If you prefer that we not exchange your name with third parties, or if you wish to clarify or modify your communication preferences, please visit us at www.ReaderService.com/consumerschoice or write to us at Reader Service Preference Service, P.O. Box 9062, Buffalo, NY 14240-9062. Include your complete name and address.

HRLP15

LARGER-PRINT BOOKS!
GET 2 FREE LARGER-PRINT NOVELS PLUS
2 FREE GIFTS!

HARLEQUIN

super romance

More Story...More Romance

YES! Please send me 2 FREE LARGER-PRINT Harlequin® Superromance® novels and my 2 FREE gifts (gifts are worth about $10). After receiving them, if I don't wish to receive any more books, I can return the shipping statement marked "cancel." If I don't cancel, I will receive 4 brand-new novels every month and be billed just $5.94 per book in the U.S. or $6.24 per book in Canada. That's a savings of at least 12% off the cover price! It's quite a bargain! Shipping and handling is just 50¢ per book in the U.S. or 75¢ per book in Canada.* I understand that accepting the 2 free books and gifts places me under no obligation to buy anything. I can always return a shipment and cancel at any time. Even if I never buy another book, the two free books and gifts are mine to keep forever.

132/332 HDN GHVC

Name	(PLEASE PRINT)

Address	Apt. #

City	State/Prov.	Zip/Postal Code

Signature (if under 18, a parent or guardian must sign)

Mail to the **Reader Service:**
IN U.S.A.: P.O. Box 1867, Buffalo, NY 14240-1867
IN CANADA: P.O. Box 609, Fort Erie, Ontario L2A 5X3

Want to try two free books from another line?
Call 1-800-873-8635 today or visit www.ReaderService.com.

* Terms and prices subject to change without notice. Prices do not include applicable taxes. Sales tax applicable in N.Y. Canadian residents will be charged applicable taxes. Offer not valid in Quebec. This offer is limited to one order per household. Not valid for current subscribers to Harlequin Superromance Larger-Print books. All orders subject to credit approval. Credit or debit balances in a customer's account(s) may be offset by any other outstanding balance owed by or to the customer. Please allow 4 to 6 weeks for delivery. Offer available while quantities last.

Your Privacy—The Reader Service is committed to protecting your privacy. Our Privacy Policy is available online at www.ReaderService.com or upon request from the Reader Service.

We make a portion of our mailing list available to reputable third parties that offer products we believe may interest you. If you prefer that we not exchange your name with third parties, or if you wish to clarify or modify your communication preferences, please visit us at www.ReaderService.com/consumerschoice or write to us at Reader Service Preference Service, P.O. Box 9062, Buffalo, NY 14240-9062. Include your complete name and address.

HSRLP15

LARGER-PRINT BOOKS!
GET 2 FREE LARGER-PRINT NOVELS PLUS
2 FREE GIFTS!

H HARLEQUIN®

INTRIGUE

BREATHTAKING ROMANTIC SUSPENSE

YES! Please send me 2 FREE LARGER-PRINT Harlequin® Intrigue novels and my 2 FREE gifts (gifts are worth about $10). After receiving them, if I don't wish to receive any more books, I can return the shipping statement marked "cancel." If I don't cancel, I will receive 6 brand-new novels every month and be billed just $5.49 per book in the U.S. or $6.24 per book in Canada. That's a saving of at least 11% off the cover price! It's quite a bargain! Shipping and handling is just 50¢ per book in the U.S. and 75¢ per book in Canada.* I understand that accepting the 2 free books and gifts places me under no obligation to buy anything. I can always return a shipment and cancel at any time. Even if I never buy another book, the two free books and gifts are mine to keep forever.

199/399 HDN GHWN

Name	(PLEASE PRINT)	
Address		Apt. #
City	State/Prov.	Zip/Postal Code

Signature (if under 18, a parent or guardian must sign)

Mail to the Reader Service:
IN U.S.A.: P.O. Box 1867, Buffalo, NY 14240-1867
IN CANADA: P.O. Box 609, Fort Erie, Ontario L2A 5X3

**Are you a subscriber to Harlequin® Intrigue books
and want to receive the larger-print edition?
Call 1-800-873-8635 today or visit www.ReaderService.com.**

* Terms and prices subject to change without notice. Prices do not include applicable taxes. Sales tax applicable in N.Y. Canadian residents will be charged applicable taxes. Offer not valid in Quebec. This offer is limited to one order per household. Not valid for current subscribers to Harlequin Intrigue Larger-Print books. All orders subject to credit approval. Credit or debit balances in a customer's account(s) may be offset by any other outstanding balance owed by or to the customer. Please allow 4 to 6 weeks for delivery. Offer available while quantities last.

Your Privacy—The Reader Service is committed to protecting your privacy. Our Privacy Policy is available online at www.ReaderService.com or upon request from the Reader Service.

We make a portion of our mailing list available to reputable third parties that offer products we believe may interest you. If you prefer that we not exchange your name with third parties, or if you wish to clarify or modify your communication preferences, please visit us at www.ReaderService.com/consumerchoice or write to us at Reader Service Preference Service, P.O. Box 9062, Buffalo, NY 14240-9062. Include your complete name and address.

HILP15